Murder on the Med

Book 7

A Dodo Dorchester Mystery

By

Ann Sutton

An idyllic Greek holiday. A murdered ex-pat. Connect the victim to your tourist party, and you have a problem that only Dodo can solve.

Dodo's beau, Rupert, is to meet the Dorchesters for the first time on their annual Greek holiday. He arrives in Athens by train and her family accept him immediately. But rather than be able to enjoy private family time, an eclectic group of English tourists attach themselves to the Dorchesters, and insist on touring the Parthenon with them.

Later that night, a body is found in the very area they had visited and when Dodo realizes that it is the woman she saw earlier, near the hotel, staring at someone in their group, she cannot help but get involved. The over-worked and under-staffed local detective is more than happy for her assistance and between them they unveil all the tourists' dirty secrets.

With help from Rupert and Dodo, can the detective discover the murderer and earn himself a promotion?

©2022 Ann Sutton

No part of this book may be reproduced in any form whatsoever, whether by graphic, visual, electronic, film, microfilm, tape recording or any other means, without the prior written permission of the author and publisher, except in case of brief critical reviews.

This is a work of fiction. The characters, names, incidents, places and dialogue are products of the author's imagination and are not to be construed as real. The opinions and views expressed herein belong solely to the author.

Permission for the use of sources, graphics and photos is the responsibility of the author.

Published by

Wild Poppy Publishing LLC
Highland, UT 84003

Distributed by Wild Poppy Publishing

Cover design by Julie Matern
Cover Design ©2022 Wild Poppy Publishing LLC

Edited by Jolene Perry

Dedicated to Mr. Bowden, my sixth-grade teacher

I am a naturalized American citizen born and raised in the United Kingdom. I have readers in America, the UK, Australia, Canada and beyond. But my book is set in the United Kingdom.

So which version of English should I choose?

I chose American English as it is my biggest audience, my family learns this English and my editor suggested it was the most logical.

This leads to criticism from those in other English-speaking countries, but I have neither the time nor the resources to do a special edition for each country.

I do use British words, phrases and idioms whenever I can (unless my editor does not understand them and then it behooves me to change it so that it is not confusing to my readers).

Titles and courtesy titles of the British nobility are complicated and somewhat dynamic through the ages. Earls, dukes and marquises have titles that are different from their family names. After extensive study on honorary titles and manners of address I have concluded that to the average reader it is all rather confusing and complicated. Earls, dukes and marquises have titles that are different from their family names which would be hard for readers to follow.

Therefore, in an attempt to eliminate this confusion, I have made the editorial decision to call Dodo's father Lord Dorchester rather than Lord Trent and her mother Lady Guinevere rather than Lady Trent.

Table of Contents

Chapter 1 1

Chapter 2 7

Chapter 3 14

Chapter 4 24

Chapter 5 34

Chapter 6 42

Chapter 7 49

Chapter 8 55

Chapter 9 66

Chapter 10 71

Chapter 11 77

Chapter 12 85

Chapter 13 94

Chapter 14 103

Chapter 15 113

Chapter 16 121

Chapter 17 131

Chapter 18 138

Chapter 19 145

Chapter 20 154

The End... 158

About the Author 165

Murder on the Med
Cast of Main Characters

The Dorchesters

Dorothea "Dodo" Dorchester - Lady Detective
Diantha "Didi" Dorchester - Dodo's sister
Lord Alfred Dorchester - Dodo's father
Lady Guinevere Dorchester - Dodo's mother
Rupert Danforth III - Dodo's beau
Lizzie Perkins - Dodo's maid

Other characters

Malcolm Cartwright - Brother to Phinella
Phinella Cartwright
Gerald Goodweather - Father of Reginald
Reginald Goodweather
Miles Penholland - Husband of Augusta
Augusta "Gus" Penholland
Detective Theodorou
Vera Fenchurch - Expat living in Greece

Chapter 1

The bite of salt in the breeze filled Dodo's lungs and the screech of gulls welcomed her back. Standing on the filigree iron balcony she looked out onto the turquoise blue ocean. To her right, stood an avenue of palm trees, casting their welcome shade onto the cobblestone quay that ran alongside the harbor full of masts and sails. The hotel, housed in the vast, stone walls of the old fort of Split, in the Kingdom of Slavs, Croats and Slovenes, was cool and comforting as an old friend.

"Oh, how I have needed this!" cried Didi as she joined her sister on the balcony of their shared room, dressed in a short-sleeved, red and white polka dot pantsuit. She tapped her bottom lip. "Only one thing could make this better."

"Let me guess," said Dodo. "Charlie."

Didi turned around and leaned her elbows on the edge of the balcony, letting her blonde head fall back so that the golden curls hung loose in the gentle wind.

"I know he has to finish his studies if he wants to become a professor, and February is right in the middle of term, but I really wish he had agreed to run away with me for a few weeks. I suppose being conscientious is a fine quality but sometimes I wish he wasn't quite so diligent." She placed black-rimmed sunglasses on her dainty nose and, not for the first time, Dodo sensed that her sister would be an instant hit on the silver screen should she ever entertain the idea. With fuchsia lips and diamond earrings, she looked every inch the iconic movie star.

"But you will have summers," Dodo reminded her. "You can plan adventures and when he does finally qualify, he can travel the whole world as a visiting professor."

"That is true," Didi replied. "But it's a long way down the road. He'll have to acquire two more graduate degrees before then."

"Hopefully he will be less tied to a schedule as a graduate student," Dodo said, leaning over the edge of the balcony to drink in the stunning port view.

Didi and Charlie had only recently started seeing each other and Dodo knew all too well the desire to be together every minute.

"One can hope," murmured Didi.

Charlie Chadworth had been a friend of theirs for years and they had all recently reconnected at a weekend party. Somehow, while Dodo had been chasing murderers, her sister and Charlie had fallen in love and she couldn't be happier.

A knock on the door heralded the arrival of their luggage and Dodo moved inside to open it.

"Do come in," she said as a gangly, young porter struggled in with their huge trunks. "Over here will do." She pointed to an alcove containing two enormous, glossy wooden wardrobes. Once he had relieved himself of his burdens, the young man's eyes locked onto Dodo, his ears turning pink. She thrust a handful of local currency into his hand as he left, rewarding him with a broad smile and gently pushing him out of the room. Lizzie would come up and unpack the things they needed for the next two days.

The grand, stone hotel dated from the 14th century but had been modernized in every possible way. Situated on an inlet of the Adriatic in the port city of Split, it was one of their mother's favorite hidden spots with its green, hilly backdrop and mousetrap lanes. Their Mediterranean holiday always started here after traveling across Europe by train. Like walking back in time, it was the perfect, relaxing start to their tour of the Greek Isles.

During the Great War, the country had passed through several hands and been off limits for the duration. It had been a sore trial for Lady Guinevere, not to be able to travel to this precious and beloved place during those frightful war years. The only acceptable, local alternative had been Cornwall where the scenery was breathtaking, but the February weather was cold and unpredictable.

Dodo loved the old-world charm of the port city, the hotel, and the hospitality of the local people. The whole family had celebrated being able to return in 1920.

"Are you ready to walk through the old town?" asked Didi, searching through her leather weekend bags for a sun hat.

"You are joking!" declared Dodo. "I've hardly caught my breath. I need a long, cold drink and a little nap before I venture out again."

"Wet blanket!" said Didi with her magical laugh. "I shall just have to go alone, then."

"Have fun," said Dodo settling into a deep, cushy armchair. "You can tell me all about it at dinner."

Travel by train was very comfortable these days but stray cattle on the line the night before had woken her up as the train stopped and started. Dodo picked up a vial of sweet-smelling oil. Since Lord Alfred Dorchester, the Earl of Trent, was a regular, the hotel management made a fuss of them and their staff by providing scented oils, sugared local fruits, and a bottle of wine. It paid to keep the wealthy happy.

Another knock interrupted them and Didi opened the door to Lizzie, Dodo's maid.

"Are you settled in?" Dodo asked her. "And are they spoiling you?"

"Just like usual, m'lady, although Enid didn't like her oil, so she swapped with me." Enid was Lady Guinevere's maid. She was sixty-three, unmarried, and completely devoted to her mistress. However, she was less enthusiastic about exotic holidays. Unlike Lizzie.

"Now, what can I do for you?" Lizzie continued.

"You can go walkabout with Didi," Dodo replied, flicking her hand. "I'm too tired after not sleeping well on the train and am in desperate need of a lie down."

Lizzie clasped her hands together with glee, eyes wild with excitement. "Are you sure? Don't you need me to unpack?"

"Absolutely sure! I can't function until I've had forty winks. There will be plenty of time for all that when you get back."

"Well, if you insist." Her maid was almost giggling.

"Come on then, Lizzie. Grab a hat and let's go!" said Didi with the energy of a five-year-old.

Lizzie and Didi disappeared out the heavy door in a cloud of happy laughter while Dodo walked over to her bags, an ache behind her eye proof of the bad night on the train. She had some headache powder in her handbag and mixed it with water from the clamshell sink. Before she reached the plush, inviting bed, another knock stopped her short. She wandered over to the door, ready to dismiss another porter, to find her mother and father standing there. Lord Dorchester looked fresh in an all-white suit, Panama hat, and a becoming smile, while her mother was draped in a white kaftan and matching turban, looking much younger than she was.

"Where's Didi?" asked Lady Guinevere, striding into the room.

"You just missed her. She and Lizzie have gone to walk the streets around Diocletian's Palace." The old part of the city was a short distance away and dated from the fourth century A.D. Its impossibly narrow, magical passageways ended in small, hidden courtyards full of colorful flowers, bustling cafés, and local musicians.

Her father took the seat Dodo had recently vacated but her mother stood in the open French windows to the balcony, the sun at her back.

"Already! I have hardly caught my breath!" declared Guinevere.

"I said the same thing, but you know how Didi is. Like a child who can't contain her elation."

"And you didn't go with them?" asked her father, rubbing his thumb along the palmwood arm of the chair.

"Don't you recall? I slept horribly on the train last night. All that stopping and starting. I need a rest before dinner."

Her mother took up the same stance her sister had adopted, leaning against the iron railing with the masts of boats in the background, and Dodo was struck by the similarity between the two women. She favored her mother more than her father, but the resemblance was not terribly strong.

"Of course, darling. Daddy and I are just going to walk along the harbor and wondered if you wanted to join us, but I can see you need your sleep. We'll meet in the restaurant for dinner at eight. Does that sound alright?"

"Wonderful!" Dodo responded.

"It's so good to be back! Come along, Alfie!" said Guinevere, pulling him to his feet. "Let's leave the darling girl in peace. She needs her beauty sleep before Rupert arrives." She ran a hand along Dodo's arm. "I simply can't wait to meet him!"

As the door swung closed behind them, Dodo fell back heavily onto the bed.

Another knock. She rolled her eyes and slid off the lavish bedspread thinking that her parents had forgotten something but was surprised when a porter handed her a telegram.

Darling STOP, she read.

Rupert! Her heart leaped. He was the only person in the world for whom she would put off her nap.

Looking forward to joining you in Athens next week STOP Miss you dreadfully STOP

Rupert had gone to Scotland on some lengthy business with his father and she hadn't seen him for a whole month. It was a revelation that a heart could ache this much without expiring.

"Not nearly as much as I have missed you!" she whispered to herself.

Will be on the train from Paddington at ten tomorrow STOP

"I can't wait." She ran a finger across her bottom lip. She was impatient for him to meet her family.

Dodo had spent Christmas with Rupert's family in Leicestershire, but he had yet to meet hers, though they knew all about him. Well, almost. They did not know that he had saved her from a kidnapping a few months before. She was still waiting for the right moment to tell her family *that* frightening story.

Arrive Athens station Thursday thirteen hundred STOP

She had his itinerary memorized and hoped the weather and tides did not delay him. She was suffering from severe withdrawals as she imagined the brilliant smile that revealed the beloved chip in his front tooth from a youthful polo accident.

Kisses STOP

He had not ended with 'I love you.' They had both stopped short of saying that so far.

But she was more than ready.

Chapter 2

The lavish, seventy-five foot, white and gold yacht glimmered in the Mediterranean sunshine, rising like a mythical mermaid out of the shimmering, aqua water of the quay. *The Queen of Sheba* was not new to the Dorchesters; they had rented her every year since she was built in 1910, except for the war years, but she had recently been refurbished. Everything about her had been upgraded and rejuvenated and she glowed, a dazzling memorial to her namesake.

Her bright, white sails snapped in the brisk breeze as gulls swept and dipped on air perfumed by sugary-sweet mimosas.

The captain led them to the indoor dining area where an artistic luncheon of seafoods had been laid out. Lizzie and the other servants went below to find their cabins.

The dining space had windows on all sides which gave a spectacular, 360-degree view of the port of Split. Dodo had finally slept well and developed a healthy appetite during the morning by walking along the ancient harbor wall. She sat and flicked out her napkin eager to begin.

As the waiter poured the traditional fizzy, sweet champagne, the captain raised anchor and the yacht glided out of the harbor and onto the open, aquamarine sea. The memory of the freezing, wet winter they had left behind disappeared from Dodo's mind like vapors of smoke.

How fortunate people were to live in such an idyllic climate, where temperatures remained mild all year long and rain was rare.

Her father lifted his glass. "To fine weather, a fine ship, and fine company!" His oversized mustache curled into a broad, hairy smile.

Everyone raised their glasses. "Hear! Hear!"

Beaming with affection at his wife and daughters he declared, "And there is no group of people I would rather spend this splendid time with!"

As the boat picked up speed, the waiters removed the remnants of the giant prawns and replaced them with lightly grilled lobster, served with an authentic Greek salad.

It was so good to be back.

After lunch, Dodo and Didi donned the latest bathing costumes from the House of Dubois and laid out on the white, kid-leather seating on the deck that was soft as clotted cream while their parents enjoyed a cocktail inside. Dodo had persuaded Lizzie to come and sit in the sun for a little while, but she soon got antsy to be up and doing and went inside to press the girls' clothing.

"So, now that I am well rested, and my headache has gone, tell me all about meeting Charlie," Dodo said as she stirred local fruit into her fresh lemonade. "I feel bad that we haven't had time to connect in a long while."

Didi's lovely face lit up. "I know! I have missed our talks. We have both been so busy socializing."

Dodo let the comment go—she had been busy solving murders.

"It was at Poppy Weatherington's birthday party," Didi continued. "I was supposed to go with a crowd of girlfriends but they all came down with the flu, so I ended up going alone. There were so many people there I didn't know, that when Gerald Thorndike rolled up and asked me to dance, I accepted."

"That buffoon! You *must* have been desperate. How did it go?" asked Dodo.

"As you might imagine. He was already three sheets to the wind and became a little aggressive."

"Can't say I'm surprised," commented Dodo. "He never did know when to stop."

"No. Well, I was getting rather desperate, when Charlie appeared like a knight in shining armor to my rescue. He pretended we were together."

"Always the gentleman," agreed Dodo.

"It wasn't that long ago we saw him at Farrington Hall, remember?" asked Didi.

How could she forget? It had been a devastating week full of murder and lost friendships.

"Of course! He rescued us when we got a flat tire in the rain."

"That's right." Didi looked out over the ocean clipping past. "He was swooning over *you* back then. I have liked him since I was thirteen, but it was as if I didn't exist."

Dodo decided not to comment since Didi was not wrong.

After several moments of reflection, Didi turned back. "Anyway, there he was rescuing the damsel in distress and looking devastatingly handsome in a crisp dinner suit. He was alone too, and we started chatting and just didn't stop. He told me some fascinating things about history—things I never learned at school."

Dodo suppressed a grin. Didi had absolutely hated history as a girl and Charlie was reading history at Oxford with hopes of becoming a professor.

"We stayed together the whole evening and then he offered to take me home. He was a perfect gentleman. I was hoping he would kiss me but he just gave me a peck on the cheek. I was crazy to see him again but he needed some encouragement. After some slight hiccups, we met up in town and he seemed to really *see* me. It was a turning point. After several more dates, he finally kissed me." She turned wide-eyes on her sister. "Oh, Dodo! It makes such a difference with someone you are wild about. The sparks could have started a forest fire!"

Dodo knew firsthand. When she and Charlie had started seeing each other in the summer, he had been a very capable kisser. He just hadn't inspired the necessary attraction in her that…someone else had. It had become extremely complicated.

"After that first kiss, we saw each other every day. The magic between us took my breath away, and we fell hard for each other. I have never felt this way about anyone. Never!" Her delightful eyes were shining, and her pretty face glowing. "Now, we just hate to be apart. As I said before, I was really hoping he could ditch his classes and come and join us for a few days, but he explained that he is at a critical juncture in his studies and couldn't possibly." Her mouth turned down in a pout that would have forced Charlie to kiss her again. "Now, tell me all about you and Rupert. I must know what changed."

Between heartaches and murders over the last few months, Dodo had been emotionally spent. As close as she and Didi were, she had not had the energy necessary to bare her soul. In fact, some of the events had actually made her quite fragile. Was she ready now?

She took off her sunglasses. "As you know, I took an instant dislike to Rupert the first time I set eyes on him." she declared, smiling at the memory. She pulled her mouth down dramatically. "You will remember he was with Veronica the Vengeful." She had told her sister a little about her escapades in Devon but now filled her in on all the juicy details about the murder at their cousins' home on the Devonshire moors. It was solving the murder that had brought her and Rupert together. Didi laughed at her spirited delivery.

"Why *did* you go to Blackwood?" asked Didi. "You never said."

Dodo wrinkled her nose. "It involves Charlie. Do you really want to know?"

Her sister laid a hand on her arm. "Of course. You are my sister and besides, all that is in the past. I want to know everything."

Dodo took a deep breath and told Didi all about her summer fling with Charlie that was disrupted by the murder at the Queen's Race and the reappearance of the enigmatic Chief Inspector Blood.

"Charlie suspected you had feelings for Chief Inspector Blood," said her sister, incredulously. "I could tell there was some attraction at Farrington Hall, but I didn't think it was anything serious."

Dodo covered her eyes. "I know! He got under my skin and did strange things to my heart— things Charlie was not doing. I realized it wasn't fair to Charlie and cut him loose."

"Were you tempted to take it farther with the chief inspector?"

"Of course, I was tempted! The man is dark and brooding and well, extremely good-looking. It took all I had not to kiss him in that broom cupboard."

Didi laughed. "I am imagining the crazy lady threatening to kill you outside, and all you can think about is wanting to kiss the policeman you are imprisoned with."

"It was not funny at the time. I thought I was losing my mind. It hurt so much to walk away from both of them. I was broken."

Didi squeezed her hand. "And that's why you ran away?"

Dodo sighed. "Yes. I had to. You know it could never have worked with the chief inspector. Too many obstacles, we are too different. It would not have lasted."

Didi shook her head. "You are right, of course. Can you imagine Daddy's face if you had brought the chief inspector home for dinner?"

Dodo smiled at the thought.

"Mummy would have loved the romanticism of defying society, but even she would have known that in the long run, it was doomed to fail."

Dodo's eyes prickled. She should have confided in Didi a long time ago. "I knew you would understand."

"And then you met Rupert," Didi continued.

"Yes. You can imagine the last thing I wanted was to meet someone. My heart was bruised and torn to shreds."

"He must have made quite an impression," declared Didi.

"Well, the first one was the wrong impression. I just about choked when Veronica arrived. So much for a relaxing week! And no man who considered Veronica eligible would interest me—no matter how striking he was."

"Is he uncommonly handsome?"

"I pinch myself every time I see him, Didi. He is like some Greek god." She giggled.

"What changed your mind about him?" asked Didi.

"As soon as he explained *why* he had come with Veronica, as payback for Veronica helping his sister, I viewed him through a different lens. Then he was invaluable in helping to solve the murder." She leaned back and replaced her sunglasses. "We arranged to meet again, and I was able to help him iron out another sticky situation with his sister. Seeing how he treated her, how kind he was—in the end isn't that the most important thing? Daddy is terribly kind to Mummy and I believe that is why their marriage is so strong."

Didi raised precisely sculpted brows. "How exactly did you help his sister?"

Even in the safety of the yacht, as the memory of her kidnapping crashed through Dodo's mind, she mentally withdrew. It was still too raw. Instead, she centered the story on the false accusation against Rupert's sister, Beatrice, and the hilarious, eccentric older neighbor who nursed a crush on Rupert.

Again, Didi was in stitches.

"With the neighbor as the competition, I was irresistible," remarked Dodo.

When Didi had stopped laughing her expression turned serious. "Do you love him?"

"I do." It was a relief to say it out loud.

"Then I can't wait to meet him."

Chapter 3

They sailed on a sea as calm as a pond and arrived in the busy port of Athens the following morning. The plan was to stay in the capital for a few days and show Rupert around, since it was his first visit to the area.

As Dodo looked out on the port, watching as they docked, her stomach clenched in excited anticipation. Today she would see Rupert! Her chest was crowded with competing emotions; elation to be with him again and nervousness about introducing him to her family. She wanted everything to be perfect…and life rarely was.

His train was due into Athens station at one o'clock. She had told her family she would meet him alone, unwilling to share that intimate moment of reunion, even with them.

Never the most patient of people, after settling into the Grand hotel, Dodo left early for the train station.

As she stood on the platform, eyes squinting against the sun, trying to get a first glance of the train that would not be arriving for another thirty minutes, she laughed at herself. The sun was high in the sky and she felt a band of perspiration around her hairline and a drop trickle down her back.

She looked around. The platform was made of marble tile and the walls were full of arched windows and doors. A small canopy sat at the back of the platform to shade waiting passengers but that did not give her a good view of the tracks. She glanced at her delicate, silver watch; still twenty minutes.

She ducked inside the empty, old booking hall where a sign declared it to have been built in June of 1884, to look for a drinking fountain. The water had an unusual taste, very different from that in the fountains in England, but it satisfied her thirst.

The ticket room was full of amber glass and dark, carved wood and the three booths were divided by intricate iron railings. Gazing up, she saw that even the ceiling was decorated with inlaid wooden beams with local, white symbols fashioned out of plaster and embedded into the crown molding.

After several minutes in the cooler building, she pushed through the doors to the furnace-like platform. Several travelers were now waiting, a young mother with two adorable little girls and a man dressed in cool, white.

Glancing at her watch for the hundredth time, she checked it against the one on a pole. Both said ten minutes to one.

The line was still empty.

Worrying the skin on the side of her thumb, she leaned to the right and took off her sunglasses. Was that steam?

No. It was a cloud.

Her frustrated gaze collided with the dark, rich eyes of one of the children. She couldn't have been more than five years old. Her lips curled into a shy smile, revealing two missing teeth. Dodo smiled back.

Looking down the track again, Dodo strained her eyes. This time the sun glinted off red metal and moving steam rose into the clear blue of the sky.

He was here!

Her heart hammered as the tiny train grew until she could see the shiny grill on the front of the engine.

Suddenly a figure popped a head out of a window.

Rupert!

His blond locks blew back from his face and he ran a hand through his hair to keep it out of his eyes.

Dodo waved madly and he leaned out farther, waving back as though he were mad as a hatter. She worried he might fall as she continued waving. Every second brought him closer and she thought her heart might burst out of her chest.

Before the train stopped, as the wheels and brakes screeched and the steam valve hissed, Rupert jumped out and ran along the platform. Lifting Dodo off her feet, he swung her round like a giddy schoolboy until she shrieked with laughter and planted a huge smooch on his laughing mouth. She pulled back to soak up the gorgeous sight of him.

Putting her down, he cupped her chin and placed a tender, delicious kiss to her lips that made her tingle from head to toe.

"You cannot imagine how much I have missed you," he breathed into her ear.

"Oh yes, I can!" she whispered back.

He grabbed both her hands, kissing her knuckles.

"Let's get your bags and send them to the hotel," she said, unable to stop grinning.

They waited, clutching each other, as a porter removed his luggage from the train and they made the arrangements to have it sent on to the hotel.

"Are you hungry?" she asked Rupert.

"Now that I am back where I belong," he put an arm around her shoulders, "I'm famished. I haven't eaten since last night."

"Me neither!" she declared.

She guided him out of the station onto the street and looked around. "There's a café. We should be able to find something to hold us over."

Once inside, they sat under a large fan, eating fresh olives and ordered taramasalata and papoutsakia—stuffed aubergine. Dipping pita bread into the sauces, Dodo asked about his journey.

"Apart from being interminably long…" His eyes widened. "It was good. Although, I did almost miss my connection in Munich when I tried to find an English newspaper."

"I'm glad you didn't," she responded. "I ran through all sorts of terrible scenarios in my head that would prevent you from arriving. I don't think my heart could have survived."

"And I was wondering if anyone had dropped dead at your feet while you were traveling?" he said, with a delightfully crooked and cynical grin. "No dead duchesses or deceased dukes?"

She swatted his arm. "You make it sound like I go looking for trouble," she lamented with a good-natured pout. "But trouble finds me!"

"I know! That's why I asked."

"We are on holiday," she remarked. "No murders allowed!"

After paying the bill they hailed a taxi to take them to the *Grand Hotel*. Dodo felt a jangle of stress. She had arranged for her family to meet Rupert in the hotel bar at three in the afternoon—a time when the bar should be quiet.

They talked of nothings and basked in being together, crushing her designer outfit in their need to be close. A part of her had been missing since they had been separated and now she was complete again. It was not that she could not function alone—it was more that she was better with him.

Rupert removed his Panama hat and ran a hand through his hair again, a tell that he was a little nervous too.

When the taxi pulled up against the curb, Dodo stepped out into the balmy air and drew in a deep breath. The palm trees were swaying in the Mediterranean breeze and people strolled lazily past. She looked up at the boxy hotel with its eight towering stories. The bottom level was made of a series of arches, the upper floor windows braced with iron railings. The outside was regal but doggedly square—its true claim to fame being its unparalleled view of the majestic Acropolis.

The grand revolving door swooshed satisfyingly as they pushed into a formal, classic Greek foyer overrun with pillars and decorative plaster ceilings. Taking his hand, Dodo led Rupert through to the bar. It was an atrium garden, full of olive trees and local flowers. Low tables, surrounded by large easy chairs, peppered the space. Only one table had occupants.

Dodo tripped across the mosaic tile floor catching the attention of her family. She watched with interest as they each laid eyes on Rupert for the first time. Didi was grinning from ear to ear and her mother's eyes widened with unadulterated pleasure. Her father's eyes twinkled.

"Mummy! Daddy! May I present Rupert Danforth III."

Didi jumped up and rushed to give him a peck on the cheek as though they were old friends. Lord Dorchester, his handlebar mustache resplendent under his thatch of wiry gray hair, stood, and when Didi released Rupert, extended his hand. Rupert grasped him firmly and Dodo's father shook his hand till she thought Rupert's teeth might fall out.

"Splendid! Splendid! Nice to meet you, my boy!" Her father slapped him on the back.

Guinevere Dorchester stood, looking like Athena herself, draped in white and gold, her hair held up with diamond clips that winked in the light, arms outstretched.

"Rupert, darling! May I call you Rupert?"

"Of course!" he replied, allowing her to give him a peck on the cheek after he kissed her bejeweled hand.

Dodo had the comforting impression that rather than being an introduction, her family had known him for ages, and was excessively grateful for their immediate acceptance. Especially since it was so different from her awful experience meeting his family at Christmas.

"How was your journey, dear boy?" asked Dodo's mother as her father motioned for them to sit. A couple of cocktail glasses and a tumbler sat on the low table.

"Pretty good to be honest," Rupert replied. "Only one delay just outside Paris due to a farmer's trap being stuck on the line. But it is a dashed long journey."

"Perhaps in the future we will be able to fly here," said Didi brightly. "I was just reading an article about the future of travel by air."

Lady Guinevere shuddered. "I doubt that very much. Those contraptions crash all the time. They will never be ready for commercial use, in my opinion."

"I have to agree with my wife on that one," said her father. "Planes are far too primitive for popular use. Mark my words, they will improve trains so that a journey that currently takes a week will only take a day or two. And they will have all the creature comforts. Planes are tin cans in the sky. No appeal whatsoever."

Dodo flashed a wry look at Rupert before saying, "What if they could make a luxury aircraft with soft seats, good food, and fine wine? Would you change your tune?"

"No!" Lord Dorchester scoffed. "Your mother is right—they fall out of the sky far too often." He rubbed his hands together. "Now son, what can I get you?"

"I'll take a small whiskey, please."

Lord Dorchester signaled the bartender who hurried over to take his order.

"Have you been to Athens before?" asked Didi on the edge of her chair, looking fresh and adorable in a peach chiffon day dress.

"No, I have never been to Greece. The farthest east I have been is Italy," replied Rupert leaning back in his chair.

"It's too bad you missed Croatia." Didi flashed a playful grin. "Perhaps next year."

Dodo flung her a warning look.

"Dodo has told me all about it. I should have loved to join you earlier, but I just couldn't get away. It sounds like a truly marvelous place."

"It's my favorite," said Didi. "And Mummy's. But here we are in Greece which is also pretty spectacular, and you have never seen any of it. We shall take you to the Acropolis tomorrow and then to the lively center of Athens. You'll love the tiny, rabbit burrow streets and friendly, colorful people."

"I can't wait," he said, reaching for Dodo's hand with a tender smile just for her.

"Tell me about your family," said Lady Guinevere as the waiter brought his whiskey.

Rupert told them about his mother and father and two sisters, and about their home in Leicestershire. He didn't tell them about his grandmother's murder or his mother's rather stinging initial dislike of Dodo, for which she was grateful.

"And Dodo tells me you have a cozy mews house in London," remarked her mother.

"Yes, my uncle left it to me. It's perfect for a bachelor and so convenient for town."

"I know what you mean. I'm sure you've been to my little bolt hole. Lovely for seeing shows and operas," she agreed.

Although Dodo had not told them too much about Rupert, wanting him to make his own impression, she *had* warned her father not to mention the war.

"And what do you do for sport?" asked Lord Dorchester.

Rupert glanced at Dodo before saying, "Polo is my main passion, but I hunt and sail too."

"Polo?" Her father squeezed one eye shut. "Any good?"

"Daddy!" protested Dodo. "What kind of a question is that?"

"Well?" continued her father.

"He is excellent," she said, coming to Rupert's defense.

"Actually, I am a solid average," Rupert said with a jolly laugh. "Dodo has never seen me play, since we met after the season ended." He quirked an adorable eyebrow at her.

"I suppose that is true," she conceded. "But I have heard from others that he is first-rate." She turned in her seat. "I think you are being endearingly modest about your abilities."

"You are biased," he said, touching her nose with a chuckle. "I assure you, I am not."

"Thoroughbred racing is my thing," continued Lord Dorchester. "I don't ride, you understand, I merely own the horses."

Dodo put her glass on the table. "Rupert and I discovered that we may have attended several of the same races but never bumped into each other. He didn't know you owned *Arabian Knight*."

"Remarkable horse!" declared Rupert.

Lord Dorchester stroked his considerable mustache. "Yes, yes. Rum thing that he lost his chance at the Triple Crown. Still, nothing gained from dwelling on what can't be changed." He put his tumbler down on the table rather heavily.

Dodo exchanged a look with Rupert and launched into a different topic. "What time are we doing dinner? I haven't even let poor Rupert go to his room yet. I was so eager for him to meet you all." She turned to him. "I bet you're dying to freshen up."

Rupert rubbed his neck. "The idea does have a certain appeal."

"Of course!" exclaimed Lady Guinevere. "How thoughtless of us. You *must* go to your room and get settled. We have made reservations for eight o'clock. That should give you time for a nap if you need one."

"Perfect," said Rupert as he and Dodo stood.

"I shall just see him to his room and come right back," Dodo told her family, eager to hear their thoughts about him.

They walked hand in hand to the elevator and Dodo looked over her shoulder. "That went well, I think."

Rupert's mouth slid into a wry smile. "Much better than when you met my family."

"Well, your grandmother's murder did put a bit of a dent in things."

"Let's hope, as you said, nothing of the sort spoils this trip," he said.

She crossed her fingers. "We can but hope."

"Oh, Dodo!" squealed Didi, when Dodo returned to her family at the bar. "You weren't kidding about his looks!"

"He is a rather pleasant-looking young man," said her mother, taking a sip of her cocktail. "Don't you agree, Alfred?"

"What? Oh, I suppose so. Should like to see him in action on his horse. Perhaps we can go to one of his matches, if that's alright with you, Dodo."

"I think it's a brilliant idea as long as you let me see one on my own first." She leaned back, whipping the hat from her head and holding it by the brim over the arm of the easy chair.

"He is rather delicious. That smile!" She giggled and Didi joined in. "I am so glad you like him."

"He makes a tremendously good first impression," agreed her mother. "It will be nice to get to know him over the next few weeks."

"He seems like an easy-going sort of chap," commented her father. "Let's see if he can hold a decent conversation."

"Alfred…" warned Lady Guinevere.

"I am not going to grill him," grumbled Lord Dorchester.

"See that you don't, darling. You *can* be a little intimidating," warned his wife.

"Me? Intimidating?"

"Yes, Daddy," agreed Didi. "You are quite the force of nature. Charlie even said so and he has known you forever."

Lady Guinevere grabbed Dodo's hand. "I like him very much, darling, and more importantly, I can see he makes you very happy."

"Good!" said Dodo, "Because I plan on keeping him around for the foreseeable future."

Chapter 4

Lizzie was in Dodo's room, sorting out her clothes for the evening when Dodo returned.

"How did it go?" she asked, eyes wide, almost as invested in Rupert's success with the Dorchesters as Dodo.

Dodo had popped into her room to wait for dinner and for Rupert to get settled but found she was far too highly strung to rest.

I should have gone for a walk.

"Smashingly!" Dodo assured her. "I think the expression that would best describe it would be 'he knocked their socks off'!"

Lizzie clapped her hands together. "I knew it! How could anyone dislike the fellow!" She had developed an innocent partiality to Rupert from the moment she had met him in Devon.

"Well, remember that *I* did, at first," declared Dodo.

Lizzie fanned the air as if swatting a fly. "But that was just because he was acting a part, m'lady. If he had just been himself from the get-go, I don't doubt you would have fallen for him sooner." She was checking Dodo's evening gown for stains.

Dodo flung an arm across the silky bed staring at the decorative fan. "I suppose so."

"I know so!" declared Lizzie. "That man is one in a million."

Dodo rolled over and rested her chin on her hands. "Should I be worried?" she asked her maid.

Lizzie shot her a look before doubling over with laughter. "Oh, that's a good one, m'lady. Very funny." She hung the dress back in the glossy walnut wardrobe. "But if I could find a man half so nice…"

"You *do* deserve your turn," agreed Dodo. "Perhaps some nice tourist will catch your eye and you can have a holiday fling. I'm sorry that being a maid gives you so little recreational time."

Lizzie closed the door to the wardrobe and faced her mistress. "For starters, I am more than grateful for my position. None of my sisters are in service and none of them get to travel to exotic locations in the lap of luxury. I am incredibly lucky, and I know it. And secondly, I'm not really interested since the last time I tried my hand at romance, he turned out to be a wrong'un." Lizzie frowned. "I don't have much confidence in my ability to choose wisely. I'm easily turned by a handsome face, it seems."

"Nonsense! That man was a confidence trickster," cried Dodo. "Everyone was taken in by him, including me."

Lizzie moved over to the dressing table and selected a long chain necklace to match the evening gown. "I suppose so." She sounded unconvinced.

"And practice makes perfect," said Dodo. "I haven't always been successful, as you well know."

Chuckling, Lizzie withdrew the curling iron from one of the cases and arranged the combs and brushes on the dressing table. "That is true," she agreed. "You shouldn't judge a book by its cover, even if it's posh."

Dodo moved to sit on the velvet, rolled arm bench at the bottom her bed. "So, you cannot give up before you've started. There's someone out there for you, Lizzie, I'm sure of it."

Finished with her chores, Lizzie stood by the door. "Will you be taking a bath before dinner?"

Dodo remembered how sticky she was while waiting for Rupert in the sun. "Yes, I think that is a good idea since I got rather hot earlier. Can you book me in for one?" Her suite had a small bathroom with a sink and private toilet but no bathtub. Those were shared by guests on each floor.

"Of course. I'll do that right now. I'll let you know what time."

When Lizzie left, Dodo leaned her head back, enjoying the knowledge that Rupert was here in Greece. She watched the fan over the bed turn as she replayed the thrill of the moment Rupert stuck his head out of the train window and their joyful reunion on the platform. Many men had passed through her life but only one other man had come close to making her feel the way Rupert did. She had never been so head-over-heels in love before, and his absence had only made her love stronger.

For the first time, she could see a future with someone. She hugged herself and squealed.

"Everything alright, m'lady?" asked Lizzie, materializing at the door again.

"I'm just deliriously happy," announced Dodo.

"Well, it's about time!" said Lizzie with a grin. "Oh, and the bath will be free in twenty minutes."

"Marvelous!"

The family had planned to meet at the rooftop bar before dinner. Dodo floated down the stairs in a new Renée Dubois creation that mixed fabric textures and feathers. A sleeveless bodice plunged to a deep 'v' in the back from whence a narrow train fell and kissed the floor. The front was gathered under the bust then fell to the ankle. Even by her standards it was stunning.

Rupert was already there, resplendent in a white dinner jacket and bow tie, his light hair held perfectly in place with brilliantine, his skin freshly shaven. She could imagine just how good he smelled.

His impossibly blue eyes widened, and a smile radiated across his face as she approached.

"What a sight for sore eyes!" he murmured as he stood, drawing her into his arms and kissing her gently under her chin.

She shivered. "I've missed that."

"Me too." His voice was silky and low and rumbled through her rib cage.

"Hello, you two!"

Dodo turned to see Didi, looking like a million dollars with her blonde curls pinned up to reveal her swan-like neck, lips red as blood.

"Stunning!" Dodo exclaimed, kissing her sister.

"You don't look too bad yourself," said Didi with a chuckle.

"Exquisite!" declared Rupert, kissing Didi's gloved hand.

"Shall we get a drink?" Didi asked as various waiters almost bumped into chairs as they stared at the two dazzling women.

"I think as soon as Mummy and Daddy arrive, we will go in to dinner, so probably not."

They sat in light gray leather club chairs that faced a bar decorated with an enormous, complex mosaic. Dodo looked around the room half full of tourists of all ages, some of them definitely British. Spotting the English abroad was something of a family sport, since they usually stuck out like a sore thumb. She easily identified a fellow countrywoman stuck in the late 19th century, her dark gray gown tasteful but outdated, her back stiff as new leather. Her husband was portly, his bald head shiny under the electric lights. They were looking in opposite directions in silence.

"Darlings!" Dodo's mother approached in a dazzling gown that was almost fashionable but fit to perfection, showing off her mother's narrow figure. Dodo was impressed. Usually, Lady Guinevere favored pre-war styles. The hem of this particular gown only reached to mid-calf rather than all the way to her ankles and was straight from the shoulders instead of cinched with a corset.

"What a fabulous dress," she said, sincerely, hugging her mother close.

"I decided to try something a little different," she responded. "Do you think it works?"

"Absolutely!" As an ambassador for more than one fashion house, Dodo was thrilled to see her mother experimenting.

Her father was immaculate, as usual, in a traditional dinner suit.

A clock chimed the hour.

"Dinner!" said her father.

As they entered the rooftop restaurant, Rupert gasped.

They had been given a table right on the edge with an uninterrupted, breathtaking view of the lighted Acropolis.

"This is just one of the reasons why we love this hotel," explained Dodo's mother.

"I can totally understand why," remarked Rupert.

As they were seated, Dodo noticed the older couple from the bar, near their table. They were still not talking.

Her father ordered some wine as a young English couple entered noisily, taking the table to the left of them. They were rather loud, and Lord Dorchester shot a look of disdain across the space like an arrow from a bow.

"My apologies," said the fresh-looking young man. "Please excuse my sister. She has had one too many pre-dinner cocktails."

The redheaded sister lifted her cocktail glass high, revealing a nasty sunburn on her freckled arms and shoulders as her wrap slipped.

"Cheers!" she cried, a few decibels too loud.

"Keep it down, Phinella," pleaded her brother. "Or they will kick us out." His bright smile squashed into a forced one.

Phinella put a polished nail to her lips and hiccupped. "Shhh!"

Her brother rolled his eyes at Dodo's table. "I shall do my best to keep her under control."

Everyone at the Dorchester table picked up their menus and tried to ignore the rambunctious, young couple next to them. As Dodo looked over the various dish descriptions, she noticed another couple who were so obviously British as to almost be a caricature. An older man in his seventies and a younger, carbon copy, who could only be his son, wearing thick, round, wire-rimmed glasses. They nodded to Dodo who acknowledged them, then continued perusing the menu.

The waiter returned with his notepad hardly able to tear his eyes from Didi in her sleeveless, silver gown.

Lord Dorchester cleared his throat.

"Ah yes, sir," said the waiter in reasonably good English. "What can I get you?"

After a wonderful dinner, the family retired to an outdoor bar adjacent to the restaurant that overlooked both the Acropolis and an enormous, lighted swimming pool.

"May we join you?" asked the older man with his presumed son who leered secretively at Didi through half-closed eyes. Dodo pushed down a wave of disgust and wished her father would refuse the request.

"Of course," responded Lord Dorchester, ever polite. He stood and offered his hand. "Alfred Dorchester, and this is my wife, Lady Guinevere Dorchester and my daughters, Dorothea and Diantha."

"Delighted," responded the older man who had a slight stoop. "My name is Gerald Goodweather and this is my son, Reginald. We are archeologists."

"Is that so?" said Rupert, extending his hand. "Rupert Danforth."

"Yes, we're here for a dig but have arrived a few days early to sample the delights of Athens."

"Where is the dig?" asked Rupert. By his tone he was an enthusiast, which was news to Dodo.

"Olympia. Important work to do there," Mr. Goodweather said, pulling up a seat for himself and his son. "I believe there are still many significant treasures to uncover at the site."

They were distracted for a moment as a waiter, who was apparently mooning over Dodo and Didi, tripped over a small table, sending the glasses on his tray shattering to the stone floor. Dodo jumped out of her skin and Rupert put a reassuring hand on her arm.

"No murderers here," he whispered into her ear.

"I should hope not!" she responded. "I'm in Greece to relax with *you*."

The waiter recovered his step, face red from ear to ear, and scraped the remnants of the glasses back onto his tray before hightailing it out of the bar area.

"Is this your first time in Greece?" Dodo asked, directing her comments to the son, Reginald in spite of her aversion.

"No, we have been to Olympia before but have never visited Athens," replied his father. "I intend to rectify that this time around. How can one come to the area and not visit the treasures of the capital city?"

Reginald avoided Dodo's eye and stared into his glass.

"Indeed," she responded, watching the son fiddle with his cuffs.

As they were all quietly conversing, the young man with the ill-mannered sister appeared, alone. "I say!" he said. "May I join you? Had to drop my sister back to the room and she was out like a light. Now I'm at a loose end with no company."

Dodo glanced at her father to see his reaction. In spite of a deep frown, manners won the day. "Certainly. Pull up a chair."

"Malcolm," the young man said, shaking everyone's hand. "Malcom Cartwright. Over from Manchester for a holiday. Can't beat the weather here in February."

"Are you of the Bradford Cartwrights?" asked Rupert. "I'm good friends with Morty Cartwright."

"No," said Malcom, the smile sliding from his lips. "Can't say that I am. My people are strictly from Manchester."

Rupert twisted his lips before taking a slug from his glass.

What was that all about? She must remember to ask Rupert later.

Engaged in small conversations with their neighbors, a shadow fell across the group. Looking up, Dodo saw the rigid Edwardian lady and her short husband.

"I recognize you all from the restaurant and conclude that you are English. I wonder if we might join you?" The woman's generous lips were slack like overused elastic bands and several, thick gray hairs protruded from her sharp chin.

"Please," said Lord Dorchester, gesturing with a sweep of his arm.

The compact husband's face transformed, filling with warm camaraderie, reminding Dodo of the description of the dwarf *Happy* in the fairytale. He dragged two chairs over to join the group. Didi, Rupert, and Dodo pushed their chairs farther out to accommodate them.

"Miles Penholland," said the husband in a surprisingly low voice. "And my wife, Augusta."

Perfect! The name suited and Dodo secretly nick-named her 'Gus'.

"We are from Sussex," Augusta drawled with the overly pronounced accent of the social climber. Dodo inwardly groaned. "We are neighbors to the Marquis of Milford Haven."

She must have found out Daddy is an earl and thought this would trump him. How insufferable!

"Here for a spot of sun, what!" Her husband seemed to be an affable chap. Life must be difficult chained to such austerity.

"Us too," agreed Lady Guinevere, with grace. "Though I love my country to distraction, I find February a little too gray. I just have to get away."

"Same here," announced Malcolm Cartwright. "Improves my mood no end. Sunshine is good for the soul."

"Hear! Hear!" said Didi.

Malcolm, who had made eyes at Didi since he joined the group, appeared grateful for an excuse to look her full in the face. With his thin, lank hair and broad forehead, he was just not in Didi's league and besides, she was taken.

A waiter approached with a silver tray held high and leaned down to present a telegram to Mr. Goodweather. As his eyes scanned the text, Dodo was sure the man's color paled, but he crushed the paper and stuffed it into his pocket, declaring, "That was from the lead archeologist on the dig. We are all set to begin next week." His statement did not match his expression.

"We're going to climb to the Acropolis tomorrow," said Didi in her charming manner. "This is Rupert's first time."

"I was thinking *we* might do that," said Malcolm, his nose quivering. "Perhaps we can join you."

Dodo's mood flagged. The last thing she wanted was a group of hangers-on for her first holiday with Rupert.

"I should think we will go quite late in the day," she said, hoping to discourage Mr. Cartwright. "I'm sure you will want to get up there early."

"Not at all," replied Malcolm, enthusiastically. "My sister is a late riser. That will work perfectly."

"Mind if we join you too?" asked Mr. Goodweather, smoothing his thinning, gray hair. For the first time a hint of interest animated his awkward son's expressionless face and Dodo saw him shoot another furtive glance at Didi. Dodo tried not to frown but was pretty sure her expression was somewhere between horror and disdain.

Lord Dorchester cast a worried glance at Dodo and very slightly tipped his head. She gave a hint of a shrug back and he barely nodded.

"The more the merrier." Only the Dorchesters knew his tone was overly hearty.

It was just one day, after all.

"In that case," droned 'Gus Penholland, "We will take that as an invitation. We had plans to go the day after tomorrow, but these things are much more fun with a group."

'Fun' was not a word Dodo would associate with the stiff Mrs. Penholland and tomorrow was beginning to look more like a punishment than a pleasure.

By a squeeze of her hand, Rupert indicated his understanding that this arrangement was not ideal but that it did not bother him. She felt grateful that he knew her well enough to appreciate that this would not constitute her definition of a perfect sightseeing trip.

She leaned back in her chair, still holding his hand and let the bubble of conversation surround her as she realigned her expectations for the next day.

Her mind wandered to the image of Mr. Goodweather crushing the telegram with knitted brow and stuffing it in his pocket. Ever suspicious, she thought, *"What was really in that telegram?"*

Chapter 5

After a morning of swimming and a lazy lunch poolside, about half of the British group was assembled in the square lobby with its elaborate, gilded ceiling, ready for their excursion to the Acropolis. Despite Coco Chanel accidentally making a tan fashionable, Dodo was all for protecting her pale skin. She smoothed the leg of her wide trousers and adjusted her straw hat. As she ran a hand down her gauzy sleeves the slight pain reminded her that she had caught a little too much sun at the pool earlier. Didi arrived, her white skirt flowing behind her looking fresh as a daisy. One hand went to her hat draped with a gauzy scarf while the other held out a parasol for Dodo.

Next to arrive, Rupert pushed through a door with combed, wet hair looking good enough to eat in his whites, which contrasted beautifully with his already bronzing skin. Dodo's heart skipped.

The previously tipsy sister, Phinella Cartwright, entered the lobby rolling her ankle in totally impractical shoes and wearing a crumpled, shapeless, linen dress that was good quality but did nothing for her figure. Her brother steadied her as she flushed to the roots of her auburn hair. Having made the climb several times before, Dodo knew that flat shoes, though not as attractive, were a must. Phinella's pasty, freckled skin was still not properly covered, in spite of the burn on her forearms. Some people never learned.

"Good afternoon, Miss Cartwright," Dodo said from behind. The girl must not have heard her as she did not turn around. Dodo cleared her throat and tried again. Her brother nudged her.

"Oh, yes. Lovely," she responded vaguely, her pale lashes sweeping her freckled cheek. Clearly, not much of a conversationalist when she was sober.

Mr. Penholland was eager as a boy scout with the familiar Baedeker's Guide grasped in his pudgy hand, while the pendulous, permanent bags under his austere wife's eyes contributed to an aura of boredom. Dodo wondered why she was even coming.

The last couple to arrive were the aging archeologist and his peculiar, myopic son, dressed as one might expect—looking more like scientists than tourists in khaki clothes and hard hats.

"Shall I lead?" asked Dodo's father. A general murmur indicated that everyone was fine with that arrangement. "Follow me then." He lifted a silver-tipped walking cane and exited the hotel, hailing several waiting rickshaws to take them to the base of the Acropolis.

As the large, eclectic group stood on the pavement waiting to hop in to the conveyances, Dodo noticed a small, elderly woman wearing a permanent scowl, crossing from the other side. Half-way across she stopped short, seeming to stare at the group of tourists. Her eyes narrowed as she slowly resumed her passage to their side of the street. Jumping into the last rickshaw with Rupert, Dodo kept her eyes on the woman who was still standing on the pavement, gazing after their caravan.

"Everything alright?" asked Rupert with concern, turning to follow Dodo's gaze.

"Yes, fine." she said, flipping her head around and tucking her arm through his. "Absolutely perfect."

Once they were all deposited at the bottom of the famous Greek hill, her father raised his cane again and the group began a slow ascent. Unfortunately, floods of other tourists had chosen to see the sight today too, and Dodo had to keep an eye on her father's cane so as not to get lost in the crowd.

"Hard to believe that something so old has survived," commented Rupert. "Amazing technology for their day."

"It's over two thousand years old," Dodo confirmed, watching Phinella struggle on the uneven surface in her heels. "I like to imagine how the people would have dressed. And togas are making something of a comeback."

Her mother and Didi were bringing up the rear as Didi took pictures with her trusty Brownie camera, while their father was at the head of the group. The father and son archeologists were walking right behind him, Mr. Goodweather talking nineteen to the dozen, followed closely by the Penhollands. The Cartwrights were just in front of Dodo and Rupert.

As the group neared the top, Dodo felt the glow of exertion under her light coverings, wishing she had brought a fan.

"If you will all gather here?" called her father, raising his gravelly voice. He was in his element being in charge, and this was a topic about which he was somewhat of an expert. If he hadn't been born an earl, Dodo could easily see him as a professor.

Once everyone was within earshot, Lord Dorchester began his lecture on the ancient structure. Rupert was spellbound but Dodo had heard it many times before and let her eyes wander. She jerked her eyes back to a distant pillar. Had she seen the woman from outside the hotel? She lifted her sunglasses to get a better look but the woman, or mirage, had disappeared.

Puzzled, she turned her attention back to her father, who was enjoying himself immensely, his large mustache moving up and down like a squirrel's tail. Nagged by the idea she had imagined the mysterious woman, she turned her gaze back to the column, but a crowd had gathered, listening to their own guide. Too much sun, perhaps?

Fifteen minutes later, her father finished his lecture and encouraged everyone to go their separate ways to explore. Two by two their compatriots split off.

"Come on," said Didi, pulling Dodo's arm. "Let's show Rupert the view of Athens from the other side.

They strode through two marble columns of the colonnade, into the interior chamber, across the ancient floor and out the front of the Propylaea. Athens was laid out before them like a huge, relief map.

"Wow!" said Rupert. "What a sight! I've seen it in books, of course, but in person it is beyond spectacular."

"There! You can see the Temple of Zeus," Dodo said, pointing. "And over there is the Plaka or ancient area of the city."

The day was clear and bright, and the vista like a giant open-air fresco that never got old.

"My sisters would love this," he said, placing an arm around Dodo's shoulders.

"What about your parents?" she asked.

"You've experienced my mother's…moods. She prefers to stay local."

"Ahh," said Dodo with understanding.

After standing in the heat for a while, surveying the tableau, Dodo suggested they go to the temple of Athena to find relief from the sun in the shade of the many columns. Wandering around to the temple, Dodo's gaze snapped to attention as she thought she saw the unknown, grumpy woman from earlier, on the other side. She slipped her arm out of Rupert's and hurried across the space, but the woman had disappeared again. She put a hand to her head.

"Hang on!" Rupert protested, catching up with her. "Where are you going?"

"I thought I saw someone…" she murmured, continuing out the other side, determined to see if her eyes truly were playing tricks on her.

Nothing.

She looked down the steep stairs on that side of the temple, a snarl of trees and bushes at the bottom.

She re-entered the ruin, searching from left to right.

Rupert's fingers touched her shoulder.

"I must have been mistaken. I think the heat is getting to me."

"Who?" asked Didi. "Someone from home?"

"No." She explained the whole scene she had witnessed as they entered the rickshaws.

"This *is* one of the biggest tourist spots in the area," said Rupert, reasonably. "It's not too surprising to see a familiar face here."

Dodo swung her gaze around one last time. "No. I suppose you're right."

The shade from the temple walls was welcome and they hovered, examining the structure, Dodo concentrating with her peripheral vision for further signs of the mystery woman. She was still not totally convinced she had imagined seeing her.

The Penhollands entered the temple and nodded in their direction as they walked the interior of the temple. His round face was jolly and red from the heat, his wife's as morose and gray as ever. They wandered around for a bit then exited on the other side down the stairs. Then the Cartwright's entered in heated conversation. When the pair saw Dodo's group, they abruptly quieted, flashed stiff smiles, and Phinella hobbled to the other side of the structure with her brother in her wake. In a quiet corner, it appeared that the previous, intense conversation was revisited.

"Ready?" asked Didi.

"Actually, I'm rather enjoying the cool shade. I think I will stay a little longer but don't let me keep you," Dodo replied.

"In that case, I am going to find Mummy. Are you coming Rupert?"

"No thanks! I'll stay in here with Dodo."

Didi skipped out of the temple and Dodo leaned against a rough column.

"I say, are you alright?" asked Rupert, peering into her eyes with concern.

"I'm fine. It just feels like I'm going a little bit lala. I was so sure I saw that woman and then to think I saw her again makes me believe I was not hallucinating. I really just want to see if she re-appears. You know how I am."

His lips curled in a charming smile, revealing the treasured, chipped tooth. "Indeed, I do. Never can ignore a mystery." He brushed a finger across her nose.

"Exactly."

Mr. Goodweather raised his hand in welcome as he and Reginald entered the temple. The son's eyes were darting uncontrollably around the space.

"What do you think of them?" whispered Rupert.

"Well, Reginald is a bit creepy. Such an odd, piggy-looking boy with those tiny eyes behind the thick glasses. Makes me rather uncomfortable, to be honest. And I would say that the only real enthusiast is the father. He drags his son along, but the son's heart is not in it."

"I agree. I haven't heard more than two words out of Reginald," said Rupert. "I saw them on the landing last night when I went to use the bath and tried to strike up a conversation with the son. It was like pulling teeth. His father answered for him in the end."

"Perhaps that's the problem—an overbearing father," said Dodo.

"Maybe." She noticed that Rupert's gaze followed the father and son as they exited down the stone stairs on the opposite side. "Don't you think it odd that a self-proclaimed archeologist does not know the history of the Parthenon?"

Dodo huffed. "I suppose so." She pulled up her parasol and opened it, taking one last look around. "Well, I think I must have been mistaken about the woman I thought I saw. Shall we catch up with my parents?"

After spending all afternoon with the ad hoc group, the Dorchesters ate dinner alone in another of the hotel's restaurants. They sat at a table for five in a secluded interior courtyard.

"What did you think of today's outing," her father asked Rupert after they had eaten.

"Marvelous, sir," he replied. "It's mind-blowing to contemplate the sheer age of the places. I should like to explore some more tomorrow. I've always loved history."

"Well, we have two more nights here before we set sail again, so there should be plenty of time for that."

"How do you feel about a tag-along?" Didi asked him. "I'm sure Mummy and Daddy will prefer to relax by the pool tomorrow."

"That would be splendid," said Rupert. "You and Dodo have both been here before and can serve as my tour guides."

"Then I suggest an authentic gyro for lunch," declared Didi. "I have been craving one since we arrived. It is rather clumsy street food made from thinly sliced, spiced lamb cooked on a spit and wrapped in traditional pita bread with cucumbers, tomatoes and the most delicious yogurt sauce you ever tasted. You'll be dreaming about them for weeks after!"

"Oh, yes!" agreed Dodo. "It's one of our favorite things to eat here. We can delve into the streets of the old town and find a vendor—"

Before she finished, a sharp cry from one of the waiters huddled round the bar caught their attention.

"Wonder what that's all about?" said Rupert.

"Probably got a bad tip," commented Lord Dorchester, stroking his mustache as his eyes slid over to the noisy men.

Dodo's mother chuckled. "I daresay."

"Ready for an after-dinner drink?" asked her father, raising an arm to signal the waiters.

Everyone at the table nodded, but Dodo's father could not catch any of the wait staff's attention. He clapped his hands but still the men were more intrigued by their conversation than coming to their aid.

"I have never experienced bad service here before," declared her father. "I shall ask to see the manager after dinner. This is intolerable."

The slight young men, in their tight, starched, white shirts, coal black trousers, and white linen aprons were flailing their arms, engrossed in the conversation and gasping at intervals.

What on earth is going on?

Five more minutes passed, and her father looked like thunder as her mother did her best to smooth his ruffled feathers.

Finally, one of the waiters detached himself from the group. "My deepest apologies," he began, his handsome face, pale and drawn. "I am now at your service."

Lord Dorchester huffed into his mustache with displeasure.

"Is everything alright?" Dodo asked him, noticing that the rest of the group still had their heads bowed in hushed discussion.

He glanced back, nervously, drumming his pencil on the small notebook in his hand. He hesitated.

"You can tell us," she assured him, the hairs on the nape of her neck standing on end.

"There has been a murder at the Acropolis!" he whispered.

Chapter 6

Watching her mother's face crumple in distress, Dodo asked, "Do you know who was murdered?"

"She well-known in area," said the waiter in rudimentary English, rubbing a finger under his nose. "She one of your fellow English, retired, no marry and stay here in Greece for winter and return for summer." He thought for a moment. "Violet? No, Vera Fenchurch. Miss."

A jolt of intelligence flashed through Dodo's brain. "I don't suppose she was in her late sixties, average height, bony with graying hair and dark eyes?"

The waiter's eyes narrowed. "Bony? I do not know this word," he said.

Dodo gestured with her elbow and pointed to the angle. "Bony. Sharp."

The waiter pointed at Dodo. "Ah, yes! Do you know her?" Surprise swept over his young, pleasant features.

"No," she explained, "but strangely enough, I think I saw her earlier today as we were leaving for the Acropolis." She tucked her hair behind her ear, attempting to rein in her curiosity and not spook the man into clamming up. "I don't suppose you know where…it happened?"

"The temple of Athena is what they saying. Stabbed in back."

Validation pumped through Dodo's veins.

Lady Guinevere let out a sharp gasp. "Oh, Dodo! Murder follows you like ants to sugar." She looked at her husband with a hand to her forehead. "I think I will go and have a lie down." She left in a state.

A thousand questions ran through Dodo's mind. "Do you know any other details?" she asked the waiter.

"No. My friend"—he jerked his head to indicate the gaggle of waiters— "has brother who work at boarding house where this Vera stay and he tell us." He repositioned the pencil. "It was big shock. I never know anyone who murdered before." He rolled his shoulders. "But I am ready to take your order now."

Though Dodo's mind had gone into overdrive, she ordered a cocktail and as the waiter went back to give the order to the bartender she whispered to Rupert, "That is the description of the woman I thought was following us earlier. What are the odds of her staring at our party and then ending up dead?"

"What woman?" asked Didi.

Dodo reminded her about the woman she thought she had seen at the Acropolis.

"As I look back, it was as though she recognized someone," she explained.

"From our group? Surely not," said Didi.

"Why would she have followed us to the Parthenon, if not? And how many times have *we* met people abroad we know from home?"

"Quite a few," conceded Didi.

"You can't be saying that someone from our group murdered her," began Rupert. Dodo gave him the stink eye. "My mistake," he said, an irresistible smile hitching the left side of his mouth. "That is exactly what you are saying."

"We need to find out all we can about these 'strangers'," she declared. "I would place good money on the fact that someone is lying about themselves. It is so easy to reinvent oneself abroad. Shed the old self like a surplus skin and slip on a new one." She was warming to the theme. "What we need to do is get these people talking, give them plenty of opportunities to make a mistake. If they are not who they say they are, it is bound to happen."

"Shouldn't we tell the police what you suspect?" asked Didi.

Dodo rested her chin in her palm. "From their perspective, I have the flimsiest of reasons for accusing any of these people." Stirring her cocktail, she continued, "I need more to go on for them to take me seriously. They will rightly think I am some meddling tourist with nothing better to do. Let's do some sleuthing and see if we can't gather more evidence first."

Lord Dorchester shook his head. "I know you are good at this Dodo, and I confess I am rather interested, but I should go to your mother." He stood, pulled down his white, linen shirt, and made a slight bow to them. "Good night, then," he said stooping to kiss both his daughters on the cheek. "And be careful."

As soon as he left, Dodo scooted to the edge of her chair. "Right, let's go and find the others."

Didi looked at the clock. "Do you think anyone will be up? It's eleven-thirty."

"We don't know until we try."

Dodo felt a little like a big cat stalking its prey.

Fortunately, there were people still awake. They found the Cartwrights up in the open-air bar. Malcolm was leaning close and whispering something into his sister's ear. When he saw Dodo, Rupert, and Didi approach, he pulled back as if Phinella were a viper.

Dodo had suggested they not relay the latest news, reasoning that if those they questioned already knew about the murder, they would surely bring it up. Relaxed conversation was preferred for her purposes.

"Hello," said Malcolm, his sister looking askance at Didi. "We missed you at dinner, tonight."

"My parents needed a little space," Dodo explained. "But now they have gone to bed, we can socialize. I think they have dancing here after midnight."

"Do they?" asked Phinella, in her voice that sounded like the high string on a violin. "I do love to dance."

"Did you eat with everyone else, tonight?" asked Rupert.

"Yes, everyone else but your family was up here in the rooftop garden," said Malcolm. "Although Mrs. What's-her-name was in a foul mood. Poor husband couldn't put a foot right. It was rather embarrassing to tell the truth. I would never allow my wife to henpeck me like that."

"I suppose when you have been married that long all the passion and tenderness is gone," said Didi.

"If there was any to start with." His sister chuckled. "She's what my mother would call a catty sour face."

It was the perfect description of 'Gus and Dodo had to stifle a smile.

"Actually, Mr. Penholland mentioned to me that they married later in life," said Rupert.

"Well, she looks like she is having second thoughts." Malcolm laughed like a hyena.

A trio of musicians started to set up on a small platform at the back of the bar.

"What are your plans for tomorrow?" Rupert asked Malcolm.

The Cartwrights glanced at each other and shrugged. "We hadn't really thought about it. Perhaps just lay around the pool."

"We are going into the old city in search of authentic street food," said Didi with enthusiasm. "You should come."

"That sounds more adventurous. What do you think, Phinella?"

"Do you mind if we join you?" she asked. "I wouldn't want to crash your party."

Dodo crossed her fingers behind her back. "Not in the least. It will be fun." It worried her a little that she could lie so easily. The last thing she wanted to do was waste the time she had with Rupert sightseeing with strangers but digging into the crime took precedence.

While they were talking, the jazz band started playing smooth sounds. Dodo slipped her hands into Rupert's and tipped her head to indicate that Didi should dance with Malcolm. Didi's eyes widened. Dodo widened hers back.

"What a lovely tune this is," Didi began. "Do you like jazz, Mr. Cartwright"

"Call me Malcolm, please. I do." There was a pause. "Oh! Would you like to dance Miss Dorchester?"

A strange tension emerged in the air that Dodo could not define.

"I'd love to, Malcolm." He took Didi's hand and guided her to the dancefloor.

Rupert slipped his arm around Dodo's waist and for a moment she forgot about everything else as he guided her to the floor. They had not danced together before.

Rupert proved to be an expert, and she allowed herself to fall completely under his spell.

Several other couples joined them on the floor and as one brushed into them she lifted her head from Rupert's shoulder to look around. Mr. Cartwright was evidently a clumsy dancer by the way he and Didi were awkwardly holding each other about a foot apart. She glanced at his sister and was surprised to see disdain etched on her face. She swiveled her head to look back over at Didi. She looked and moved like a starlet. His sister must be giving in to jealousy. Frankly, looking at the pale, mouse of a girl, Dodo couldn't blame her.

Rupert rested his cheek on her head and she lost track of everyone else again.

When the music stopped, she felt the loss, wanting it to go on forever. Then she remembered they had work to do.

She tugged Rupert gently and they reluctantly returned to the bar.

Miss Cartwright had turned her back to the floor and was dipping into her cocktail rather heavily. Dodo hoped she wasn't going to get drunk again.

Didi and Malcolm also returned. Dodo threw her a quick mouth shrug.

"I must apologize again for stepping on your toes," he said to Didi.

"Think nothing of it," said her sister, rubbing her foot. "It was probably my fault."

The band struck up another tune, but no one suggested dancing. Instead, they found seats around a low table with several candles throwing out soft, flickering light.

"What do you do in Manchester?" asked Rupert, addressing Malcolm.

"Oh, this and that," he replied. "I'm a bit of a dabbler." He threw the rest of his cocktail down his throat and wiped his mouth with a vulgar swipe of the hand. "Bit of speculation, stocks and the like, and a sliver of real estate."

"Stocks?" exclaimed Dodo. "Perhaps you know my friend David Bellamy?"

"Bellamy? Bellamy?" Malcolm shook his head. "Doesn't ring a bell. Like I said, I only dabble."

"Another friend of mine played at the stock market last year and got caught up in the Teapot Dome Scandal," she said.

"Ah yes. Africa, wasn't it? Terrible," remarked Malcom.

"I'm feeling rather tired," said Miss Cartwright. "What time will you be venturing into the old city tomorrow?"

"Around noon, I should say," said Dodo. "Will that work for you?"

"Certainly. We'll see you in the lobby. Goodnight. Let's go, Malcolm."

As the two of them departed the bar, Dodo said, "Well, that was enlightening."

"It was?" said Didi and Rupert together.

"Our Mr. Cartwright is a fraud. That man knows less about the stock market than I do!"

"What do you mean?" asked Didi.

"Don't you remember Freddy Farrington's little money problem that led him to commit murder?"

"Yeeees," replied Didi, slowly.

"He had invested in the Teapot Dome Scandal. It was in America not Africa," she said with the same pleasure a magician has when pulling a rabbit from a hat.

"Right," said Didi. "I wonder why Mr. Cartwright felt the need to lie about what he does?"

"Good question," agreed Rupert, "and since we are on the subject of Malcolm Cartwright's authenticity, this has been bothering me since yesterday. Everyone in the Midlands knows the Cartwrights of Bradford city. How could he have the same last name and not know them? And Manchester is not that far from Bradford."

"Is this enough to report your suspicions about them to the police?" asked Didi.

"Not really. But it is fishy. It certainly puts him at the top of my suspect list," said Dodo.

They waited around a bit longer to see if any of the other vacationers appeared but no one did.

Didi stretched and yawned. "I think I'm going to turn in."

After she left, Rupert guided Dodo to the floor again. She slid her arms around his neck.

"Do you really think Malcolm Cartwright had something to do with the murder?" Rupert asked.

"I'm not sure yet, but their lies throw a cloud of doubt over them," she replied.

"It's somewhere to start, anyway," said Rupert.

"I love it when you talk murder to me," whispered Dodo.

Chapter 7

"There has been a murder," murmured Dodo from the comfort of her bed the next morning as Lizzie came to wake her.

As was often the case when Lizzie was surprised, her manners slipped. "Blimey! You've only been 'ere five minutes!" She crossed the plush Turkish carpet in nothing flat and sat on the bed beside her employer.

Dodo hoped her smile indicated that she was well aware of the irony. "Certainly not what I was expecting on a holiday with my parents. Mummy is very disturbed by it."

"I shouldn't wonder," responded Lizzie, placing a tea tray on the bed as Dodo pushed herself up to sitting.

It was well understood by everyone in the family that Lady Guinevere avoided nastiness if it were at all possible.

"Was it someone from the hotel who was murdered?" Lizzie asked.

"No, but it was a person some of the staff knew. She's a British retiree who wintered in these parts. But Lizzie, I saw her before she died!"

Dodo told Lizzie about noticing the victim, Miss Fenchurch, as they left for the day of sightseeing and how she thought she had also seen her up at the Parthenon.

"Dare I ask how?" said Lizzie.

"It's actually rather gory," said Dodo. "She was stabbed near the temple of Athena. She wasn't found till the evening. I suppose it would be a quick thing, but the killer took a heck of a risk. The place was literally crawling with tourists."

"How terrible."

"Not a bad retirement plan though, wintering in Greece each year. Mother would love it," said Dodo.

Lizzie began to arrange the cosmetics on the dressing table. "How did you find out?"

"The wait staff were clearly preoccupied with something last night after dinner as they were not performing their duties. Daddy was getting rather heated about it and spoke of talking to the management to complain when one of them apologized and explained why they had been distracted."

"Are you thinking it was someone from your group?" asked Lizzie. Dodo had described the people who had attached themselves to the Dorchesters in her usually caustic and hilarious fashion.

"It is the most logical conclusion since the woman, Vera, appeared to recognize someone enough to follow us up to the Parthenon to confirm her suspicions. I'm guessing she was killed to keep her from revealing something."

"And you saw her up there before she was murdered?" asked Lizzie.

"At the time I couldn't actually be sure as I would get a glimpse of her one minute and she would be gone the next. To be honest, I thought I might be seeing things from too much sun. Obviously, her murder confirms that I was not."

"But you'll leave it for the police to sort out, right, m'lady? It would spoil your holiday with Mr. Danforth and besides we set sail in a couple of days."

Dodo gave her maid a side glance. "You know I can't," she moaned. "I find sleuthing so irresistible…and you must confess I'm pretty good at it."

"There is no contradicting that, m'lady, but think of your poor mother. Consider how it would ruin the holiday."

Dodo's eyelashes swept her cheek.

"You've begun already, haven't you?" Lizzie's tone was that of a mother telling off a child who has stolen a biscuit.

"I told you, I can't help myself. And in any case, I doubt the police will let us leave since we are part of the group. In their eyes, *we* are also suspects, though all three of us can give each other an alibi. But I do think it is time to give the police a statement."

"In that case, you might as well tell me everything. I know it helps you get it all straight in your mind," said Lizzie, sitting on the soft stool next to the dressing table, hands on her knees.

"Well, there's the fact that Miss Fenchurch stared at our group then followed us and ended up dead, for starters. Then, we found the brother and sister, the Cartwrights, at the bar last night, before the details of the murder were public. Mr. Cartwright claims he dabbles in the stock market, so I tested him."

"How did you do that?"

"I made reference to the Teapot Dome Scandal that Freddy Farrington got mixed up in and Malcolm Cartwright thought it was in Africa. Africa! Ignorance of that shows he knows nothing about the stock market. So, the question is, why did he feel the need to lie about his occupation?"

"That *is* interesting," Lizzie agreed, watching Dodo put sugar in her tea.

"*And* he didn't know David Bellamy. *Everyone* in stocks knows David. Which reminds me. I need to get a message to him."

"Well, you can't call him from here. You'll have to use the telegraph," Lizzie pointed out.

"That's what I was thinking. Do you suppose I can do it from the hotel? I did receive one from Rupert in Split."

"I'll ask and let you know. You might be able to telephone the telegraph office."

"I wonder if the rest of our traveling companions are hiding anything," Dodo continued, taking a sip of the tea. "My past experience tells me that they are."

"You will wiggle the secrets out of them, m'lady. You always do."

"Are you dressing Didi?" she asked.

"Lady Diantha said she would take care of herself. I think she's used to doing everything herself since she has never hired her own maid. Do you think she ever will?"

Dodo slipped out of bed, wrapped a silk robe around her, and replaced Lizzie at the dressing table. She dipped her fingers into some cold cream and dotted it around her face. "I don't know. Didi is independent in that domain in a way I never was. She seems to think the whole system of servants is on its way out."

Lizzie caught Dodo's eye in the mirror. "Do you, m'lady?"

Dodo sighed. "There are certainly more options for people in the way of work these days." She pivoted on the stool. "But I would miss you."

"I'm glad to hear it, though…"

Dodo was about to apply some face powder but snapped her eyes up to meet her maid's. Lizzie's cheeks turned pink.

"Has something happened, Lizzie?" She clapped her hands. "Have you met someone?"

"Yes and no," Lizzie said evasively.

"Dish!" demanded Dodo, forgetting about the murder and her beauty routine. She pointed to the armchair and Lizzie sat.

"It's probably nothing," she began, twiddling her fingers. "But there is a young valet who attends an elderly gentleman from Devon, and he has been extremely kind to me."

"Is he handsome?" Dodo asked.

"Well, he's nothing like Mr. Rupert, of course, but *I* think so. He has kind, warm eyes and carries his suit very well." The pink was spreading from her cheeks to her neck, evidence that she was underplaying the level of attraction.

"Oh, Lizzie! And you did it all by yourself!" cried Dodo.

Lizzie raised a palm. "Hold your horses, m'lady. I'm not sure if there *is* anything there yet."

"Well, what has he done?" Dodo demanded.

Lizzie's round eyes turned dreamy. "We met when we bumped into each other as we were both getting hot water to do some spot cleaning. Since we were both in service, I struck up a conversation. He offered to carry my water up the stairs for me."

"Very chivalrous. Have you seen him since?"

Lizzie stuck her hands in her pockets. "He walked me to my room and asked if we could have lunch around the same time. We ate together while you were in Athens and chatted like old friends. He is so easy to talk to."

"Sounds promising. What's his name?" pressed Dodo.

Lizzie clasped her hands under her chin. "Ernest Scott. Ernie to his friends."

Dodo was pleased as punch. "And where are his people from?"

"He is one of four boys who were born in Exeter. His oldest brother died in the war and his youngest works on the railway. He and the other brother are both in service."

Dodo could feel her face split into an uncontrollable smile.

"What?" demanded Lizzie.

"You know a great deal about him for someone you just met. Perhaps staying in Athens a few more days for the murder investigation will work in your favor." She leaned forward. "When can I meet him?"

Lizzie's hands dropped to her sides, her face serious. "Oh, m'lady! You can't! It wouldn't be proper."

"But perhaps I could bump into him, if I knew where he might be," suggested Dodo.

A line formed between Lizzie's eyes. "I forbid you to spy on him, m'lady. If he found out he'd ditch me for sure."

Dodo stroked her chin. "You're probably right. But I simply must have a little peek."

Lizzie's mouth twisted. "I'll see if I can arrange it," she said reluctantly. "But I'm not promising anything."

"Of course. But I shall be terribly impatient now," Dodo complained. "You know how I get. I shan't rest till I have given my seal of approval."

"You make it sound like we are getting married next week," said Lizzie, offering Dodo the rouge. "It was just lunch."

Dodo wagged her finger at her beloved maid. "You never know."

Chapter 8

Though Dodo felt a responsibility to run over to the police station to give her statement, she was anxious to question more of their group first and thought she might succeed in finding some of them at breakfast. Having dressed in a simple frock with a gauzy, embroidered duster over the top, she scouted the restaurants and soon found the Penhollands.

"Mind if I join you?" she asked.

'Gus's prune-like face said no, but her tight lips said, "Of course, we'd be delighted."

I'd hate to see what your 'not delighted' expression is.

Taking a different approach from the night before, Dodo asked, "Did you hear the news?" She flicked a large, Egyptian cotton napkin onto her lap.

"News?" asked Mr. Penholland, his brow forming high arcs under his bald pate.

"There was a *murder* at the Acropolis!" She tried to infuse the sentence with her best tattling tone.

'Gus narrowed her steely, dark eyes at Dodo.

"We don't indulge in gossip," she hissed, placing her cup deliberately in its saucer with a crisp smack.

"Oh, it's not gossip," said Dodo, trying to look horrified at the very thought. "It's a fact."

A waiter floated to the table and Dodo ordered an omelet and orange juice. "I don't suppose you have croissants?" she asked before he left.

"The finest in Athens from an old French bakery," he replied.

Then I'll take one of those too, and some hot chocolate." French breakfast was one of her favorite vices.

"A fact?" asked Mr. Penholland. "Is it in the morning papers?" His gaze swung around the room as if the murderer was going to pounce on his porridge.

"I would wager it is," Dodo responded.

Mr. Penholland flagged another waiter. "Do you have an English edition of the newspaper?"

"No sir," he replied. "But I can get you a Greek version and translate for you."

Miles Penholland's head bobbed up and down. "Let's do that."

The young waiter disappeared and returned with the paper. Splashed across the front page was a large picture of the dead woman alive and well, and a small picture along the bottom of her dead body, face down in the grasses behind the temple of Athena. The color drained out of Mr. Penholland's cheeks.

"Do you need me to translate, sir?" asked the waiter.

"No," he responded. "The pictures are clear enough. Thank you."

The waiter withdrew.

"Let me see that," said his wife, stretching a stick thin, wrinkled arm across the table.

Her husband's mouth pulled down into a frown. "I don't think that would be a good idea, dearest," he resisted. "It will put you off your food."

"Nonsense! I am not some lily-livered youngster," she retorted, snatching the paper from his hands.

Dodo watched her carefully but other than an initial synchronized flaring of her nostrils and eyes, 'Gus's face merely hardened, and her eyes narrowed. She was clearly made of stronger stuff than her husband.

"Should I know her?" 'Gus asked, handing the paper back to her husband as Dodo tried to catch another glance of the picture.

"Apparently she's a regular here during the winter," Dodo explained. "Returning to England for the summers. She is quite familiar to the locals."

"Was she staying here at *The Grand*?" 'Gus asked, buttering some toast.

"No, but she was known to some of the staff."

The waiter returned with a light, yellow omelet and the crispy croissant. Dodo's mouth began to water. She took a delightful bite of the pastry and wiped the golden flakes from her mouth.

"But *I* saw her yesterday," continued Dodo.

"Saw her?" asked Mr. Penholland. "At the hotel?"

"Yes. Well, no," said Dodo. "She was crossing the road as we were leaving the hotel and I saw her again at the Acropolis."

"That's rather a coincidence," said Mr. Penholland.

"Not really," said Dodo, after a silky gulp of the creamy hot chocolate. "She was following us."

'Gus put down her knife and fork and glared at Dodo. "Why on earth would a total stranger be following us?"

"*That* is the golden question," replied Dodo, with a sweet smile. "Why indeed?"

'Gus took a huge bite of her toast, her ample jaws working with rhythmic precision. Dabbing her lips for crumbs, she said, "Well, it is of no consequence now, if she's dead."

"On the contrary," Dodo contradicted. "If I were a policeman, I would ask myself why an English woman who followed a group of English tourists ended the day dead."

Any color left in Mr. Penholland's face faded. "Are you saying you believe the police will question us?"

"Certainly, I can guarantee it, since I will be giving them my statement that I witnessed the woman, Vera Fenchurch, stop and stare at our group as we left, and then follow us to the Acropolis."

Both Penhollands fixed her with a horrified glare.

"Why would you do that?" he complained, rubbing his shiny head. "None of us knew the woman, and it will only cause us to be delayed. We have a schedule to keep. We can suffer no delay. We are to head over to Egypt tomorrow to tour the pyramids."

"Because it is the right thing to do," said Dodo with conviction.

'Gus's eyebrows were doing the quickstep. "They cannot stop us, Miles," she protested, her long nose quivering. "We have absolutely nothing to do with this. I think it is an infringement of our rights. They cannot prevent us from continuing on with our holiday."

Dodo watched the increase in indignation with interest. "I think you will find they can," she said.

"I shall complain to the British embassy!" declared 'Gus.

"Do what you must," said Dodo, experiencing an urge to dunk her croissant in the milky hot chocolate but thinking better of it in the present company. "But that will make the case even bigger by drawing the attention of the British government and delay you further, in my opinion."

'Gus growled. "This is just our luck!" She placed a wrinkled, arthritic finger to her head. "I have a headache. If you will excuse me." She pushed her chair back roughly and stomped from the room. Her husband watched and then turned sheepish eyes on Dodo.

"I apologize for my wife's behavior," he began. "She has looked forward to seeing the pyramids for years," he explained. "It is the holiday of a lifetime. Such a shame to have it disrupted in this way."

Dodo leaned back. "Not as unfortunate as it is for the poor victim," she pointed out.

His full, chapped cheeks reddened. "Ah, yes. I didn't mean that to sound heartless."

He aimlessly stirred his cup that was completely empty.

Dodo finished up the omelet and used her fingers to catch every flake of the croissant, watching Mr. Penholland who seemed to have entered another sphere.

"I should go and see to my wife," he said, eventually. "Please excuse me, Lady Dorothea."

"Of course."

He pushed back his chair and followed in his wife's footsteps.

Dodo had certainly put the cat among the pigeons. She sat thinking about the interaction when Rupert appeared looking fresh and fabulous.

"There you are! I've been looking all over for you." His soft lips touched hers sending electrical charges up and down her spine.

"I just had a rather interesting conversation with the Penhollands," she said

Rupert's top lip hitched up. "So *that* is why you are up so early."

Dodo blinked slowly. "You can't blame a girl. Asking questions as soon as possible after the crime is vital."

Elbows on the table, his big blue eyes held hers. "And what did you learn?"

She recounted the conversation.

His mouth twisted. "I hate to be a contrarian, but I think their reaction is perfectly natural. How will your parents feel about a delay in their plans?"

Dodo huffed. "I suppose you are right."

"Sorry to burst your bubble, old bean," he said, taking her hand and surveying the empty plates on the table. He raised a hand to alert a waiter.

"No, it's fine. I was feeling a little too self-satisfied. I should not give their reaction more weight because I don't like them." She ran a finger down his perfect nose. "You are my other Watson."

"Other Watson?"

"Yes. I have already knighted Lizzie as my first."

"Well, that makes sense. She has been with you longer."

A waiter arrived and Rupert ordered a full English breakfast. "What other plans do you have for today?"

"I am going to the police station to give my statement before someone kills me." She flashed her eyes at him.

"What?" cried Rupert in alarm, slamming the table with his hands. "Have you been threatened?"

It was comforting to know he was so concerned for her welfare. "No! Goodness! At least not yet, but I just told the Penhollands that I am off to tell the police what I saw. In time, everyone in the group will know and since I believe one of them to be the murderer, they might try to stop me. Remember, I am the only one who has witness testimony. I am the key. If I kept my mouth shut, it is doubtful the police would ever connect our group with the victim."

"Then I am not letting you out of my sight. If anyone tries anything they will have to get past me."

"Oh, how lovely." she declared. "What time is it?"

"Just after nine," he replied.

"Then we'd better get going. Come on!" she cried, starting to get up.

"But I haven't eaten yet," he pointed out.

"It's all in a good cause. Remember we are meeting the Cartwrights to go to lunch later. You can look forward to that."

Rupert rolled his eyes and looked longingly in the direction of the kitchens before following her out to the front curb where she hailed a taxi. They jumped in.

"Police station!" she demanded.

The driver raised a finger in the air, nodded, then proceeded to ignore every street sign in sight.

Dodo clutched Rupert as they careened round corners and narrowly missed old women on tricycles.

"I say!" she cried, but the taxi driver turned a toothless grin on her, nodding all the while. "Look at the road!" she bellowed as a mother pulled her children from the curb to avoid sudden death.

As quickly as he had screeched away, the driver slammed his foot on the brakes and threw them both forward. Dodo hit her forehead on the seat in front of her.

"You pay him! I might slap him," she said, stumbling out of the battered car holding her head.

"Me wait?" asked the driver.

"No!" they both yelled as Rupert handed him some coins. They watched in horror as he screeched away.

The police station was an old, unloved, three-story building with shutters hanging from one hinge. Inside, pungent drunks were scattered on various broken-down chairs and old ladies with deep wrinkles, licked cracked lips as they squinted into the dim light.

Dodo and Rupert waited behind a middle-aged man who was yelling at the policeman on duty while the officer yelled back. When they were done, they both shook hands and the man left.

"What was that all about?" asked Rupert to no one in particular.

"Parking ticket," explained the officer.

"You speak English?" Rupert asked.

The policeman held his finger and thumb about an inch apart. "Little."

"I have information about the murder," Dodo declared.

"Information?" he asked with his hands.

One of the men in the seats behind them was reading the newspaper. Turning, Dodo held out her hand and the shocked man placed the paper in it. She pointed to the picture of the dead woman on the front page.

The policeman pointed straight at Dodo. "You? Confess?"

Dodo shook her head violently and pointed to her eyes.

"Ah! You see who?"

Dodo pushed out her bottom lip and shook her head. "Does anyone speak English?"

The policeman held up his hand in the universal gesture for 'wait' and disappeared.

"I thought he was going to throw you in jail for a minute," said Rupert with a wry smile, hands in his pockets looking like he was out for a day of watching cricket rather than in a seedy Greek police station.

"I was beginning to think the same thing," she said with a chuckle.

The police officer returned with a man in his late forties, smoking a strong cigarette and wearing a wrinkled, pale suit. He extended a less than clean hand.

"Detective Theodorou," he said, in a sandpaper voice.

"Lady Dorothea Dorchester and Mr. Rupert Danforth." She took a deep breath and shook his hand. Rupert did likewise.

"You are here about the murder?" he asked in excellent English with little accent.

"Yes," said Dodo with relief and a query on her face.

"My mother is English," he explained. "Please, follow me."

They trailed him down flagstone hallways with thick stone walls and into a windowless, barren room with a spartan table and three rickety looking chairs. The stale air reeked of smoke and Dodo had to stop herself from grimacing. Smoke from the detective's cigarette floated toward her and she coughed.

"Please, sit," said Detective Theodorou.

He took down their names and other details and then asked what they knew about the crime.

"So, you did not see the actual murder?" he asked, chewing on a pencil that had seen better days.

Dodo shook her head and explained how they had not learned about the murder until late the night before.

Theodorou leaned back in his chair, hands behind his head. "You think she recognized someone in your group and they killed her?"

"I am afraid I do," she replied. "It is too much of a coincidence, don't you think?"

The detective rubbed his rough cheek with his palm and nodded. "What are their names?"

She and Rupert gave the names of their fellow travelers and the detective picked up an ancient phone, spitting a tangle of Greek words into it. Dodo and Rupert shared a shrug.

"I have sent a policeman to the hotel. Due to your statement, I am not letting any of them leave. He will explain things to them."

"Even for lunch?" asked Dodo.

"Yes, that's ok. I meant they cannot leave the city."

"Good," said Dodo. "Because we plan to question the Cartwrights at lunch."

The detective held up a hand. "Whoa! Why are you questioning suspects? That is best left to us."

Rupert explained about Dodo's experience in crime solving, and her connection to Scotland Yard.

"Scotland Yard?" Theodorou repeated with a look of respect.

"You can check with Sir Matthew Cusworth if you want to verify my claims," Dodo said.

He thumbed his nose. "Oh, I have no doubt you are telling the truth, Lady Dorothea." He drew a circle on the desk with the pencil. "Perhaps we can collaborate," he suggested. "I am rather short staffed, and we are not used to murders of ex-patriots here."

"I would be delighted," she said. "And in that case, you should know that I already told the Penhollands of my intention to make a statement. I wanted to gauge their reaction."

"If you believe someone in the group is the murderer that was an unnecessary risk," replied the detective. "What is your conclusion?"

"They were both more concerned that their holiday would be interrupted. Neither one showed any sympathy for the dead woman at all."

Theodorou scribbled a few notes.

"Can you tell us more details about the murder," she asked, "since we don't read Greek?"

He made a pyramid with his fingers. "Vera Fenchurch was found as the sun was setting by an employee who was securing the area before closing the attraction for the night. The victim was on the south side of the temple of Athena, rolled under a bush. The employee struck her with his boot, otherwise she would still not have been discovered as the body was well hidden. Our doctor said she appeared to have been there about four hours, which fits nicely with your testimony, and had been stabbed with a narrow instrument."

"Not a knife?" she asked.

"Definitely not a knife. The incision site was much too narrow. She was struck in the heart from the back and would have died instantly."

"Do you have an idea what it was?" she asked.

"At this point the doctor is not comfortable making a definitive conclusion. Could be a hatpin or a knitting needle or any other number of sharp, narrow items."

"Well, that's understandable," she commented. "As soon as he has settled on an opinion, I would be grateful if you could let me know."

The detective grunted. "And they knew exactly what they were doing," he continued. "Right through the ribs. She would have made little noise the doctor reckons."

"Do you know anything about the woman's personal life?" she asked.

"Other than knowing she was English, we are still gathering information."

Dodo nodded. "I do have more facts on our suspects, if you are interested."

"Of course!" replied the detective, his cigarette bouncing in his lips, dropping ash onto his suit trousers.

"Mr. Cartwright claims to be a stockbroker but knows nothing about stocks."

"And how do you know this?" he asked, narrowing his eyes as the smoke from his cigarette drifted past his deeply lined face. They told him of their conclusions from their conversation with the brother and sister the night before.

"So, this Mr. Cartwright is a fraud. Why? What is he hiding? After I have finished up my paperwork, I shall bring them in for questioning."

"And if we find out anything over lunch I'll give you a call," she said, as they stood to leave.

He held out his hand again but when Dodo reached to shake, he held her hand still in his, holding her gaze. "How do I know that *you* are not the killers, come here to direct suspicion away from yourselves?"

"I'm glad you asked, detective," she said, maintaining eye contact. "Rupert and I were with each other the entire time, and my sister was with us or my parents. You can check with them, of course."

"I intend to," he said with a sly smile, letting her hand go. "But seriously, you must be careful, Lady Dorothea," he warned. "This is a cold-blooded killer who took a great risk. I have no doubt he would readily kill again."

Chapter 9

The day was hot and the shadow of the rabbit warren, narrow lanes of Athens was welcome. In places, the lanes were so tight they had to walk in single file. Every so often, they would encounter a tiny courtyard, full of bright flowers and small groups of children playing with homemade balls and gaping at the finery of the fashionable young women. Didi stopped to take their pictures.

Dodo was using a small handbag attached to her wrist by a strap, knowing that thievery here had been elevated to an art form. She had warned Rupert against putting his wallet in his back pocket.

There was a particular restaurant that she and Didi had in mind which was frequented by the locals, the original spices not being diluted to suit the palette of European tourists.

"Is it much farther?" asked Miss Cartwright, holding onto her hat as her own bag swung from her wrist and eyeing the locals suspiciously.

"Just around the next corner," Dodo assured her.

The restaurant was located in a similarly confined alley but amazingly had a scant line of tables, sitting outside the open windows, that took up more than half the lane. Each small table was covered in bright, red and white checkered cloths.

"Here we are!" Didi declared.

They all crowded round two of the tiny tables, the men crunching their knees under the low surfaces as the tables rocked unsteadily.

"You like this place?" asked Malcolm incredulously, eyeing the surface as if he might catch some disease.

"Wait till you try the food," Dodo assured him. "Completely authentic and utterly unforgettable. I guarantee you will be telling your grandchildren about it."

A friendly, wide man in his fifties stepped out and the group let Dodo and Didi order for everyone.

"The tangy sauce on the lamb is simply incredible," Didi said dreamily.

As they waited for their food, Greek women walked by, dressed simply, with colorful scarves over their dark, thick hair, their eyes resting a moment longer than was polite on the English women's fashionable dresses.

"You're sure we're safe here?" asked Phinella, her eyes alive with concern.

"Quite sure, and besides we have these two strapping men with us." Though Mr. Cartwright could hardly be described as such.

"Speaking of safety, did you hear about the murder?" asked Didi, as they had pre-planned.

"Murder? What murder?" Phinella's thin fingers clutched her throat and she looked up and down the alley as though the murderer was poised to strike her next.

"It's all over the papers. An English woman who winters here in Greece was stabbed at the Acropolis. While we were all there, actually." Dodo watched their expressions at this revelation, deliberately leaving out the new information about the sharp, narrow weapon that had been used.

Miss Cartwright's hand now flew to her mouth. "How terrible! The very idea! And in broad daylight!"

"While we were there, you say?" asked Malcolm. "Wouldn't someone have heard something?"

"Not if the killer struck with precision," remarked Dodo. "A quick thrust in the right place and it would be over with little more than a groan."

"Dodo!" warned Rupert with a frown. "This might not be the perfect topic of conversation right before we eat."

She puckered her lips and shrugged. "Oh, sorry. How tactless of me."

"You have to excuse her," Rupert continued, addressing the brother and sister. "She's something of a sleuth. Forgets that the rest of us are more sensitive to that type of thing."

"Really?" asked Malcolm. "You are the daughter of an earl and have experience with crime solving?"

"More than you might imagine," said Didi with a sunny laugh. Malcolm's gaze lingered on her.

The waiter returned, his tray laden with five pita bread sandwiches, stuffed to the gills with thinly sliced lamb, drenched in the spicy, white yogurt sauce. Dodo grabbed hers, held her head to the side and took a delicious bite, her eyes closing with rapture. When she opened her eyes, she was happy to see everyone else tucking in.

"By Jove!" exclaimed Rupert. "I can see why you like this place so much. My tongue is exploding like fireworks night!"

"It really is rather good," echoed Malcolm, wiping sauce from his chin.

They talked of the food for some time, then Malcolm asked, "Where exactly did the murder take place?"

"Just below the temple of Athena," explained Dodo.

"I suppose it was a random mugging gone wrong," said Malcolm.

"On the contrary," began Dodo. "It appears the woman, Vera Fenchurch, was targeted." Unless they were very good actors, neither one of them recognized the name.

"How do you know so much about it?" Malcolm asked.

Dodo explained what she had witnessed and took a swig of water. "I've actually already given a statement to the local police, since I made the connection."

"We went to the temple," admitted Phinella.

"Everyone did," said Dodo. "Rupert and I were enjoying the reprieve from the heat and we saw everyone in our group come into the temple except my parents."

Phinella closed her eyes, slight lines appearing on her clear forehead. *Her light lashes would benefit from mascara.* "You said she was killed below the temple?" she finally said. "I saw both the Penhollands and the Goodweathers step through the temple and out to the other side. I was leaning against the wall fanning myself."

Malcolm shifted in his seat. "Are you accusing them?" asked her brother.

"Not at all. I cannot see what possible motive they would have to kill a stranger, but I did see them venture below the temple. It is the kind of witness the police would find very valuable, is it not?"

"It is," responded Dodo.

"But how would you feel if one of them was arrested for the murder on your testimony?" her brother asked.

"Simply awful," Phinella replied.

"But we cannot let a murderer get away scot-free because we might hurt someone's feelings," Dodo pointed out. "Believe me, I have solved crimes on the slightest of remembrances or comments."

"But to suspect anyone in our group seems outlandish," cried Malcolm. "They are all completely harmless."

"It is the only logical explanation," assured Rupert. "This woman followed our group up the hill and then was found dead. The chances that a random person killed her is unreasonable with that evidence in play."

Malcolm huffed. "I suppose when you put it like that."

Phinella pushed her unfinished gyro away. "Do you think the police will question all of us?"

"Certainly," said Dodo. "Detective Theodorou told us that no one will be able to leave Athens until the investigation is complete. I am sure there will be a message for you along those lines, when you get back to the hotel."

The two siblings shared a look that Dodo could not interpret.

"Well, that's not a problem," said Malcolm. "We had no plans to leave until next Wednesday, anyway."

"That's right," said his sister, quietly, her jaw tensing under her freckled skin.

When everyone was done, they paid the bill and wandered around the lanes to browse the various market stalls. After a short time, Phinella complained of a headache.

"I think it's the heat," she said. "I'm just not used to it."

"I'll walk back with you," said her brother. "Thank you so much, Lady Dorothea. This was quite enchanting. I doubt we would have experienced the real Athens if we had not come today. Ta-ta."

They watched the pair until they were rounding a corner, amused as a local woman tried to sell them some lace. They ignored her and disappeared around the bend.

"What did you think?" asked Dodo.

"Are you casting them as the murderers?" asked Didi, running her fingers over a pair of kid gloves on a nearby stall.

"You know me, I cast everyone as the murderer until I am faced with a fact that proves it cannot be them," said Dodo.

"She said she saw the Goodweathers and the Penhollands step through to the other side of the temple," Rupert pointed out.

Dodo tutted. "You are giving her too much credit, Rupert darling. You have to be skeptical of everything anyone says. We only have her word for it. Until someone corroborates her statement, we must consider it a lie."

"Why would she lie?" he asked.

"To deflect the attention away from herself, of course!" said Dodo.

Chapter 10

A new guest had arrived at *The Grand* with seven trunks and cases, blocking the lobby. The whole place was in an uproar. Dodo decided to beat a hasty retreat for her room but the clerk waved at her over the top of everything.

"Lady Dorothea, a telegram has arrived for you," he said, waving it in his hand.

She took the envelope with a smile of thanks and headed for the elevator.

"Who's it from?" Rupert asked.

"My friend David Bellamy. I telephoned the telegram company early this morning. I'm surprised he got back to me so soon. You haven't met David yet, but you simply must. He's the one with all the scuttlebutt."

Rupert nodded. "I remember the name. He's helped you a couple of other times."

Dodo threw up her hands. "He is better than any gossip rag."

They reached their floor, which was also full of guests and staff carrying food trays and baggage and sidled through the masses.

Arriving at her door she said, "Come in and I'll read it to you."

"Will your reputation be able to stand it?" he asked, a smile curling his lip.

She looked at him sidelong. "I am delighted that my reputation is so important to you, darling, but I'm pretty sure Lizzie will be in my room."

"In that case, carry on," he said as he followed her in.

"Good afternoon," said Lizzie brightly as she hung various dresses in the wardrobe. "I've just finished spot cleaning these. Is there anything else I can do for you, m'lady?"

"As a matter of fact," said Dodo. "You can stay and listen to David's telegram."

Dodo sat on the bed and the other two took the easy chairs.

"I asked him for any information about the Cartwrights for obvious reasons, and the Goodweathers."

"Why the Goodweathers?" Rupert asked.

"I have a vague recollection of an article that said the Olympia dig lost its funding, so I asked him to check into it. If that is so, unless Mr. Goodweather is actually Rockefeller, they are lying about why they are here." She found a letter opener on the desk. "And I've had my suspicions about them from the start. Don't you think they look too much like everyone's idea of what archeologists *should* look like? And what archeologist dresses the part even when they are not actively on a dig? It's like they are trying too hard."

She opened the envelope. *"Darling Dodo."* She looked up to see a slight frown on Rupert's face. "He calls everyone darling," she assured him and shared a quick glance with Lizzie.

Malcolm Cartwright phony STOP No Cartwrights in game STOP Goodweathers STOP Cannot confirm lack of funding for dig yet STOP Still looking for article STOP Rumor of scandal concerning son STOP need more time STOP be careful STOP

"Well!" declared Rupert. "That confirms my skepticism. Malcolm Cartwright is a fraud. He most certainly should know Morty Cartwright if he's really from Manchester. He must be using a false name." He leaned forward, elbows on his knees, right brow quirked. "This David seems awfully concerned with your well-being."

"He might have a teensy crush on me," she said, feeling a little guilty.

Rupert sat up straight.

"But you have absolutely nothing to worry about. He is just a friend. And I agree with your conclusion." said Dodo, deflecting the hot topic with flattery. "When I first spoke to Miss Cartwright, she did not react when I called her name. Everyone instinctively reacts to their own name, even in a crowd. That must be why she didn't—*it's not her real name*. Now we need to find out who they really are and why they are traveling under assumed names."

"And how are you going to do that?" Rupert asked.

"I'm not sure," she said, gripping her chin. "But I'll come up with something. Now that it is confirmed Malcolm knows nothing about the stock market, perhaps I can set a verbal trap and force a confession." She strode around the room. "Or I could get Didi to do it. He seemed to be very interested in her. Did you notice?"

"Oh yes!" replied Rupert. "That first night he could hardly take his eyes off her." He began to pace. "But according to your friend, your instincts about the Goodweathers are spot on, too. I shall see if I can find out more about the dig in Olympia on this end. There is sure to be an archeologist on staff at one of the museums here that will know." He looked at his watch. "It's probably too late now. I'll go first thing."

After dinner, the Dorchesters gathered at the rooftop bar again. Dodo had brought Didi up to speed on everything before dinner but since her mother was present, the current conversation was of the mundane rather than the murder.

"How much longer do we have to stay in Athens, Alfie?" she asked her husband.

"Don't know old thing, but until the police say we can go we are rather stuck."

"There are worse places to be stranded," she conceded.

Since her mother had opened the door, Dodo asked, "Have the police talked to you?"

"Yes, while you were gone. Very informal but they did tell us not to leave," said her father.

"The scruffy detective was rather charming," said her mother. "Hardly like a policeman at all." Dodo could well imagine the effect her mother would have on the surly detective.

"They haven't talked to me yet," said Didi.

"No, nor the Cartwrights," said her father. "I told them you had all gone out to lunch. I expect they will get round to them soon enough."

"We played bridge with the Penhollands," said her mother. "What an odd couple they are! He is so open and friendly, and she is like some dried up old spinster. Though she is the better bridge player."

Realizing that cards would be the perfect setting to learn about people, Dodo asked, "Did they have anything interesting to say?"

"Not really. Augusta is the most dreadful snob. She dropped names the entire time we played. It really was most tiresome."

"They didn't tell you anything about themselves?" she prodded.

"They did mention this is their tenth wedding anniversary," said her mother.

"Is that all?" commented Didi. "They must have been jolly old when they got married."

Skirting the topic of the murder, they went on to talk of the food they had eaten for lunch and while Didi was telling their parents about the gloves she found while shopping in the market, the Greek detective arrived in a state of some agitation.

"Good evening," he began, bestowing a glowing smile on her mother. "Lady Dorothea, I understand you toured the old city with the Cartwrights this afternoon."

"We did," she replied, wondering how best to tell him the things she had learned from David's telegram.

He rolled his shoulders. "Did they mention an engagement of any sort this evening?"

She, Didi and Rupert all looked at each other in confusion. "No, I don't believe so," she replied. "They left us early because Miss Cartwright had a headache. I assume that is why we did not see them at dinner."

The detective wiped his damp brow with a graying handkerchief. "This is not good." He murmured. "I have knocked on their door several times already with no answer. I shall have to get a master key for their room. There is always the chance that they are having an early night." He bowed. "I shall not bother you anymore. Good evening." His brow was furrowed deeper than a farmer's field, and he left before Dodo could update him.

The talk resumed but Dodo's mind was not in it.

"I'm feeling done in," said Lady Guinevere, after a while. "Coming, Alfie?"

He squeezed her hand. "I think I shall stay up a bit longer, darling. Shan't be long, though."

Lady Guinevere waved as she swept over to the elevators. Dodo's father leaned forward.

"Found out anything, Dodo?"

Rupert looked at her in surprise and she shrugged. "As a matter of fact, we have deduced that the Cartwrights are using an assumed name." She explained their reasoning.

Her father scrunched his eyes. "In their defense, I can think of several reasons a person might do that which are perfectly innocent," he said. "Especially abroad."

"Such as?" asked Didi.

"Perhaps they are famous and want to travel incognito," he suggested.

"I hardly think so," said Didi. "I think I would have recognized them since I subscribe to most of the society magazines."

"Perhaps they were accused of something at home but were cleared and came to Greece to put it behind them," their father continued.

Didi's lip curled up in disagreement. "Maybe."

"Or their parents could be infamous, and they don't want to be associated with them," suggested Rupert.

"What about—" Dodo's conversation was interrupted as the detective hurried over to them, waving his arms in the air.

"Whatever is the matter?" she asked him.

"The Cartwrights have disappeared."

Chapter 11

"What do you mean, they've disappeared?" Dodo asked, her mind running in a million different directions.

"As I told you, I got the master key and their room is empty. The beds have not been slept in. They have fled!" He put his hand to his head and dragged it over one eye.

"Could something have happened to them?" she asked, a pit of concern opening in her stomach.

"I don't think so," the agitated detective replied. "Their passports are gone and there is no money left in the room. Most of their clothes and cases are still there. I believe they have done, what is the English phrase, a bench?"

"A bunk," she corrected him.

"Yes. A bunk. Then I must ask myself, why would innocent people run?"

Dodo cleared her throat. "And I was going to tell you earlier, but you were so pre-occupied, we have just concluded that they are using an assumed name."

"What?" Theodorou shouted.

Dodo cringed. "I only received confirmation late this afternoon from a source in England, that no one by the name of Malcolm Cartwright is a stockbroker and Rupert has a friend of that name near Manchester and Malcolm said he didn't know them. The two things together led us to this conclusion."

The detective dragged his fingers through his unruly hair, eyes flaring. "Then I think we have our murderers. If you will excuse me, I shall call the station and have them circulate their description to all the ports and stations. My men need to conduct a thorough search of their room." He ran off.

An urgent itch to have a look at the so-called Cartwright's room, hit Dodo like a junkie needs a fix, but she was wise enough to understand that she was not in England and the rules were different here—even the unwritten rules.

Rupert chuckled and she looked at him in a daze. "What?"

"You look like you're fighting a craving," he said.

She raised a brow. "You think you know me that well already, huh?"

"You forget that I have a sister who is an addict. I recognize that bone-deep, desperate longing."

Now it was Dodo's turn to laugh. "You're right, of course. I am desperate to search their room but prudent enough to know I need to wait until after the police have completed their inspection. It might even be wise to ask permission."

"I certainly don't want you ending up in some dingy, Greek jail cell because you stuck your nose in where it shouldn't go," agreed her father. "Even though I know you are more than qualified."

"Ooh! That is a good point, Daddy," she gasped. "I shall be sure to keep my inquiries inside the lines."

That said, she could not stop her intelligent mind from working overtime. The circumstantial evidence was piling up against the brother and sister and it wasn't much of a stretch to conclude that they may have struck the woman in a fit of desperation to keep their true identities a secret.

An idea popped into her head. "Did you happen to take a picture of them, Didi?"

Her sister put a finger to her lips. "I was mostly taking pictures of the courtyards and ruins, but I may have got them in a shot or two."

"I hope so! Of course, I can't send the blessed thing to David even if you did, but it might be useful for the police here."

"I shall get the film developed first thing tomorrow."

"Well, there is nothing I can do, so I'm off to bed," said Lord Dorchester, smoothing his moustache. "Shall expect an update in the morning, though. And I suppose I should alert the captain that we will *not* be leaving as scheduled."

The girls kissed their father and he shook hands with Rupert. "Keep these girls in line," he said with a wink.

"Will do, sir!" Rupert replied.

They dropped back into the immensely comfortable club chairs as they watched him stroll away.

"Well!" declared Didi. "Are you surprised the Cartwright's have run away, Dodo?"

"I am," confessed Dodo. "Though I did not believe Phinella had a headache this afternoon. I thought they were just tired of our company. But if they are in hiding, a police inquiry would reveal their deception. They probably realized they had no choice."

"You don't think they are the murderers?" asked Rupert.

"They certainly have a motive, but they were too composed at lunch. I don't think Phinella would have been able to keep it together through that type of charade if they had just killed an old lady in cold blood." She tapped her toe on the floor. "No, it is more likely that they committed some crime in England and just found the situation here too hot. Though their lies and flight have certainly shone the spotlight on them."

"They *were* both in the temple of Athena," countered Didi. "And I saw them exit on the side where the murder took place. Phinella did not mention that when she said she saw the others over there. Do we know the exact time of the murder yet?" asked Didi.

"Detective Theodorou said they are placing the time of death between two, when we arrived and I caught a glimpse of Miss Fenchurch, and just before closing at five. I am not sure how sophisticated the forensic system is here, and it was very hot and would have increased decomposition. They may not be able to be more specific."

"Wait a minute," said Rupert. "We can narrow it down more than that. You saw Miss Fenchurch a little after two, Dodo. And then you saw her again. What time was that?"

Dodo let her glossy head drop back as she considered. "We got to the top and I saw her while Daddy gave his little talk. That probably took around twenty minutes, then we wandered." She twisted her mouth. "I should say around half past two."

"Too bad none of us looked at our watches," said Didi.

"That's one of the nice things about vacations—you don't have to keep looking at the time," remarked Dodo.

Rupert was scrunching his eyes and looking past them. "I did! And if the murderer is someone from our group, as you think, then the woman must have been murdered before we left. I glanced at my watch as we headed back down the hill. It was a quarter to four."

Dodo's body tightened. "So, between half past two and a quarter to four! That's rather clever of you, Rupert." She took a sip of her drink. "But it doesn't really help us, as you and I or Didi were witness to everyone in the group passing through to that side of the temple within that time frame. Everybody is still a suspect."

"Drat!" declared Didi.

As they sat feeling unresolved, the detective reappeared, rushing toward them, his dark eyes shining in triumph, waving something in a white handkerchief.

"I think we have closed the case!" he declared, beaming.

Dodo fixed her eyes on the detective's hand.

He dropped his voice making sure no one else was around to hear. "We found the murder weapon in the Cartwright's room." He opened his palm to reveal an innocuous looking hatpin. "It was hidden under the mattress. They must have forgotten about it in their haste.

Let's pray my alert will lead to finding them before they leave the country."

Dodo frowned. The Cartwrights, or whatever their real names were, had a five hour head start and could certainly be out of the country with new identities.

However, she said, "That is a coup, detective. Congratulations! Now, have you and your men finished with their room?"

His head snapped to look at her. "You don't agree that they are the killers? What more evidence do we need?"

"I admit that this is pretty damning, but we were just discussing their conduct at lunch. I hardly think they would have been able to keep so calm with us when we brought up the murder if they had just murdered the woman. They don't appear to be hardened criminal types who would kill without a second thought."

Detective Theodorou looked a little crestfallen. "I must go where the evidence leads, Lady Dorothea."

"Indeed, but I have a little latitude. Would you humor me, detective?" She pouted a little. "Would you mind terribly if I had a quick look at the room?"

He turned to putty. "I believe it is a waste of your time," he said, his fingers bunched by his temple. "But as you wish."

"Thank you, detective." She flashed him her patented smile. "Oh, and we have narrowed down the time of death a little more." She relayed their deductions. "Not that it is much use, but at least you can put it in your report."

"I certainly shall. Along with noting that the brother and sister are the culprits." He wrapped the hatpin back in the cloth and scuttled off.

"Poor man! You took the wind right out of his sails," said Rupert with a chuckle.

"He may yet be proved right," she responded. "A hatpin would certainly be thin and deadly enough and was one of the suggestions made by their medical man. But to find the item in the room seems a little…convenient, don't you think?"

"Perhaps," Rupert agreed.

Dodo stood. "Ready?" she asked.

"To comb through their room?" asked Didi. "It seems a little intrusive."

"Nonsense. The so-called Cartwrights have brought this on themselves. But unlike the detective, I am not convinced by the hatpin. I think searching their room could prove fascinating."

Didi scrunched her nose. "You can tell me all about it tomorrow," she said, yawning. "I'm off to bed."

Dodo fixed Rupert with a raised brow.

"Count me in!" he said. "It satisfies my nosy nature."

"Then we are a match made in heaven," she responded, allowing Rupert to guide her to the elevator. "I believe they are in room 204."

Rupert slid his arms around her waist and whispered into her neck. "And how do you know that? The detective did not say."

"I may or may not have looked at the registration book. I'm pretty good at reading upside down."

"You are incorrigible!" he declared, kissing her behind the ear and sending pleasurable ripples all through her.

"I know!" She turned and planted a kiss on his lips as the doors to the lift opened. "But I'm adorable!"

"I'll have to agree with that," he said, gently placing a warm hand on the small of her back and maneuvering her in.

Arriving on the second floor, she saw that there was nothing outside room 204 to indicate that it had been the scene of a search. Dodo pushed down the handle, but it was locked.

"Bother! We'll have to go and see if we can sweet talk the key out of someone," she groaned.

Rupert held his hand out, palm up. "Give me your hairpin."

She stared at him wide eyed.

Looking sheepish, he explained, "I was the champion at breaking into the tuck shop after hours at boarding school."

Dodo chuckled. "Had I known you were a petty criminal…"

"You wouldn't believe the things I learned at school that were not on the curriculum."

She glanced at him sidelong. "I think I'd rather not know!"

He knelt down and stuck the pin in, twisting it with his long, able fingers until there was an audible click. "There we are!" He stood, as the door cracked open and handed her back the hairpin.

"Impressive! I have a skeleton-key kit, but I have not learned how to use it yet," she said. "Perhaps you could teach me?"

"I'd love to," he said, placing both hands on her hips and waddling through the door behind her.

The room was smaller than hers, with two single beds separated by an olivewood nightstand containing a clock and two glasses. Both beds were neatly made, as the inspector had pointed out. A tallboy was on the wall facing the beds, containing a vase full of local blooms. Two windows looked out on the pool with the Parthenon in the background. There was no balcony.

She opened a glass-fronted wardrobe, identical to the one in her suite. Several conventional sundresses hung on the right side, while trousers and shirts hung on the left. She put her hands into one of the dresses and found a laundry label. It had the initials F.L. embroidered into it. She felt a jolt and her pulse started thrumming with energy as she looked into the men's clothes. Fingering the collar of one of the shirts she found a similar label with the initials M.L.

"What are we looking for?" asked Rupert, examining the rug.

"I've already found something!" she declared.

Rupert left the rug and came to the wardrobe, where she showed him the laundry labels.

"This confirms they are using false names," she said with excitement. "These are their real initials."

"Well done!" he said, kissing her cheek.

"Let's keep going."

Rupert strode over to the tallboy dresser and opened the top drawer revealing frilly, silk underwear. She laughed as his hand flew out of the drawer as though the knickers were hot coals. "I'll leave that drawer for you." The top of his ears were tinged pink.

Dodo ran her hand quickly under the beds with no result. She tried again, stretching her arm and fingers as far as she could reach and touched the edge of something. Shifting her position to get better leverage, she extended her arm farther and felt something like a thick paper wedged behind the nightstand. She stood up and walked around the bed and reaching down the back of the furniture piece, wiggled her fingers until they caught on the stiff paper. It was just out of reach to get a good grip. Withdrawing her arm, she regrouped and tried to move the nightstand, but it was fixed to the floor. She reached in again, pushing her shoulder hard against the wall. This time she was able to grasp the paper between her middle and index finger. She carefully pulled her arm back up, keeping her fingers tight so as not to drop the paper.

"Got it!" It was a photograph.

As she turned the picture over, her brows rose. "Well! That *is* unexpected!"

Chapter 12

"What is it?" asked Rupert, his hand in a drawer of socks.

Dodo walked over and showed him the photograph she had found.

"By golly!" he exclaimed. "I see what you mean. That *is* rather cozy."

The picture was of Phinella Cartwright, and her brother Malcolm, engaged in a passionate kiss.

Dodo flopped onto one of the beds. "This means we need to disregard everything they have told us. Clean the slate."

"Well, I think we can safely start with the fact that they are *not* brother and sister," Rupert chuckled.

"Yes, and that being the case, their sharing of a room would cause a mild scandal. Reason enough to use aliases."

"Two, young, single people on holiday together, sharing a room. That would definitely be frowned upon," he agreed. "Especially in a classy place like this."

"I doubt the hotel would have even let them stay if they knew. *The Grand* prides itself on being a respectable establishment."

"What if Vera Fenchurch knew them from England, recognized them, and threatened to reveal their secret? It would likely get them kicked out and publicly humiliated," said Rupert.

"It's a sound theory but..." She sat on the nearest bed. "Though I am known for saying people commit murder for the flimsiest of motives, it just doesn't seem enough, in this case," she protested. "And this room is spotless. They were very careful, even though they left in a hurry. That being the case, how could they have forgotten to remove the murder weapon? The only reason they left this picture is because it had fallen back against the wall out of sight. They will curse when they discover they left it."

"And you were right, she did fabricate the headache to give them time to get away," Rupert said.

"Yes, it was when we mentioned that the police would need to question everyone that the mood changed. They knew they had to leave or be unmasked. I really think it is just a case of needing to keep their identity a secret."

"So how do we explain the hatpin under the mattress?" Rupert asked.

"Let's think this through," she began. "If you had committed a murder with a hatpin, what would you do with it?"

He pulled his ear as he thought and shuddered. "I'd wipe it on the grass and put it back in the hat."

"Exactly!" Dodo cried. "Every woman has hatpins. You would hide it in plain sight not under a mattress for the police to find."

Rupert took the photograph. "So, you are saying it was planted."

"I am. I don't believe they even knew it was there or it was placed there after they left." She got up and started to pace. "Either the murderer saw them leave in a hurry and slipped in here before the alarm went up or—"

"—or the murderer came in here while we were at lunch."

"You're catching on my darling." She kissed him. "If it was the first instance, they took an enormous risk."

"Whichever theory is correct, I am very confident that it was planted. They took all their important things. There's no way they would have forgotten to take the murder weapon, especially since they have to know their flight makes them look guilty."

"Should we take this to Detective Theodorou?" He held up the photograph.

Dodo looked at the time. It was after two in the morning. "The police are setting up a search for the people we know as the Cartwrights. Finding this picture will not make any difference to that. I think it can wait till tomorrow."

As Dodo was getting ready the next morning, she filled Lizzie in on their evening escapades and showed her the photograph.

Dodo expected her delicate sensibilities to be offended but instead, she tapped the picture and said, "Well, that makes sense, then."

Dodo spun on the seat to face her maid. "What makes sense?"

"A couple of days ago, Ernie and I were in the staff area when several of the housekeeping maids came in giggling. We thought nothing of it until a Greek lady's maid explained that they were giggling about the goings-on in one of the rooms."

Dodo's eyes widened. "Was it the Cartwright's room?"

"You guessed it, m'lady. Ernie asked what they found so funny and the maid said the housekeepers were laughing because only one bed had been slept in. Both beds were messy, but the maids had been doing this long enough to know when a bed has just been made to look like it was used. I was so shocked, I didn't know where to look. The very idea! I thought it was just idle gossip but now that you say they were not really brother and sister, it makes a lot more sense." She pulled down her bottom lip. "Still scandalous!"

Dodo tightened the robe around her. "It is rather," she agreed. "And the fear of exposure because of a police investigation into the murder, would give them reason to run away before they were outed."

"It would." Lizzie began to busy herself with tidying up. "What are your plans for today?" she asked, as Dodo applied some moisturizing cream.

"First, I need to take this photograph to the detective in charge of the case. I believe they have been looking for the so-called Cartwrights all night long. I want to find out if the police succeeded."

"In that case, I'll have you wear something more business like," said Lizzie, already flicking through the contents in the wardrobe which reminded Dodo of the laundry labels; F.L. and M.L. Finding the shocking photograph had pushed that information out of the spotlight. The detective would be very interested in that, too.

Poor Detective Theodorou was as rumpled as a discarded fish and chip wrapper. He looked up at Dodo and Rupert with red eyes and a heavy five o'clock shadow. His mood was gravelly.

"What are you two doing here?" he asked.

Dodo ignored his question. "I take it you had no luck finding the Cartwrights," she concluded.

Detective Theodorou leaned his arms heavily on his desk. "Correct! Up all night again for nothing."

"Are there no other detectives who take the night shift?" she asked.

He lifted rheumy, dark eyes. "No. It's just me. We're not used to murder here, Lady Dorothea. Petty theft and corruption is more our line and it can always wait until the next day." He ran a hand down his face. "But this case could earn me a promotion if I do it right. So there's no rest for me until the culprit is in handcuffs."

He rang a small, tarnished bell on his desk and a slight, graying woman poked her head around the door.

Theodorou snapped at her in Greek. "A man needs his coffee," he explained.

"Well, I think I have some information that will help to rouse you," she said.

"Really?" His exhausted face perked up.

As Dodo withdrew the photograph from her handbag, the woman came back with a very small cup of the blackest coffee known to man. After testing the temperature, Theodorou downed it in one gulp, wiping his lips with the back of his hand.

He sighed. "As soon as that hits my bloodstream, I shall be charged for the day."

Dodo slipped the picture across his desk. He raised an eye. "Interesting."

"I should say this is proof the Cartwrights are not siblings. And a clandestine relationship would explain the need for false names."

He tapped the picture. "There is a further complication though. I checked with immigration. They had to show their passports and the immigration staff confirmed that the documents listed their name as Cartwright. If it was merely the scandal of licentiousness"—he crossed himself— "I don't think they would have gone to the bother of paying for false passports. That takes their conduct to a whole new level."

"In order to procure those, they would have to mingle with some pretty dirty people," said Rupert.

Dodo raised her brows.

"There's a whole underground network of counterfeiters in London," he explained. "Pretty shady people. You have got to really *need* to go to them to take the risk."

Dodo's mind filled with a whole host of questions that were not appropriate to ask in the detective's office, but which she would shelve until later. She thought of the time she, Didi, and Lizzie had gone to an underground, illegal betting area for information for a case. She shuddered at the memory.

"I am aware," she replied. She turned her attention back to the detective. "So you're thinking it's more than just a naughty holiday."

"Yes. There had been a lot of premeditation before coming to Greece," said Theodorou.

Rupert shot a hand in the air. "What if they are spies?"

Rupert and Dodo had met during a case that involved a British spy who was a go-between for Germany and Britain.

Dodo sucked her cheek and considered. "I suppose the Cartwright name could be their disguise and if you, the police, started asking the wrong questions, it would blow their cover." She tapped the desk with a polished nail. "Are you authorized to contact British intelligence and make inquiries?" she asked Theodorou.

One tired eye scrunched. "Not me, but I can ask the commissioner to inquire. I'll do that as soon as we are done. However, regardless of your feelings on the matter, having found the hatpin in their room, they are currently our number one suspects, and we will want to know every detail about who they really are."

"About that," began Dodo. "How do you know the hatpin you found is the actual murder weapon?"

His face fell even farther. "That is a problem. Our lab has looked at it under a microscope and it does not contain traces of blood. But any murderer worth his salt would have been careful to wipe it clean. I am confident that a jury would still easily put the pieces together."

Dodo ran a finger along the edge of the desk. "And you don't find it the least odd that they would leave the very thing that would condemn them? It's almost as if they didn't know it was there." She locked eyes with the detective.

Theodorou's mouth flattened and he looked like he was about to growl. "Much as I do not like to admit it, that is a valid point. You are suggesting that the true murderer planted the weapon in their room."

"I think it very possible."

The detective rubbed his ample nose. "They are my best lead at this point, so I'm going to run with it. I have to report my progress to my betters and your theories are just muddying the water without another good suspect." He cracked his neck making Dodo quiver. "But if it turns out they are spies and murdered this woman as part of some intrigue, then your government will have a lot of explaining to do."

"Is it too much to ask you to let us know once your people have contacted British Intelligence?"

He gestured to his dismal office. "As you can see, I am very understaffed here, so I'll let you know if anything comes of that. Your help may prove valuable."

"Thank you." Dodo stood to leave, and Rupert followed suit. As they made for the door, she remembered something. "I suppose your police searchers noticed the laundry labels in the clothes the Cartwrights left."

A slight hesitation by the detective indicated that they had not. He made a show of looking through a notebook that was worse for wear. "Uh, I cannot seem to find any notes on that. Remind me."

She told him the clothes hanging in the wardrobe contained the wrong initials and he wrote them down on a crumpled page. "I shall share this with the commissioner when I ask him to contact your foreign office." He looked up. "Now, is that all? I have a lot to do."

"How are you so familiar with the counterfeit underground?" she asked Rupert as soon as they were back on the street.

"It's actually a funny story," he began, threading her arm through his and placing his hand over hers as if they had been carved that way in heaven. "A chap called Rummy from school showed up at my door at the mews one day."

"Rummy? I hope for his sake it's a nickname," said Dodo swallowing down a guffaw.

"He was an odd boy, with some peculiar habits, and someone called him a 'rum one' when we all arrived at age eight. The name stuck and he became Rummy. Anyway, he showed up at my door at three in the morning about a year ago and elbowed his way in, looking over his shoulder the whole time. He was frantic.

"I sat him down and plied him with a calming brandy which eventually kicked in. He explained that he had been in the underbelly of London because he needed a fake shareholder's certificate but didn't have all the necessary funds to pay for it. He told the counterfeiters he was good for the rest but folks like that are not known for their mercy, and he had to grab the counterfeit product and decamp. They sent the heavies after him and he had spent the better part of the night running away. He was pretty sure he had shaken them when he thought of hiding out with me until the rats went back to their underground dens."

"What lovely friends you have," Dodo remarked.

"Not a friend, really. But I was interested in his experience and he told me all about it. It is a thriving industry, apparently."

"There is so much about you I don't know," she murmured with a smile.

"Ditto," he retorted.

"So, you don't know me as well as you thought you did! Good! That way I can keep you interested." She touched the button of his nose. "Now, what shall we do while we wait for Theodorou's report? I know! We haven't questioned the Goodweathers yet."

"You really don't believe it was the Cartwrights or whatever their names are?"

"I really don't, and I like to be thorough!"

Chapter 13

The hotel had more occupants than it had since the night they'd arrived, and each of the restaurants was bustling. Failing to spot the Goodweathers at the first two, Dodo and Rupert succeeded at the third but were told that the restaurant was full.

"Let's grab something from the bar and watch for them to leave," suggested Rupert. "We can pretend that we meet them by chance."

They waited quite some time but were finally rewarded and waved the father and son over. They had shed the uniform of archeologists and were dressed in dinner suits. Reginald looked like an uncomfortable penguin. He looked at his father, who nodded and then the pair threaded their way through the tables, Reginald pushing his circular, wire spectacles up his round nose.

"What have you two been doing?" asked Dodo in her most jolly voice. "We haven't seen you since our visit to the Acropolis."

Mr. Goodweather put his elbows on the arms of the chair and made a bridge with his hands. "There are several museums of antiquities in the area. We've spent a lot of time researching for our dig, haven't we, Reginald?"

"What? Oh, yes." The son had difficulty maintaining eye contact, and Dodo began to wonder if he suffered from some sort of social anxiety.

"Did you find anything particularly interesting?" asked Rupert.

"Certainly. There are displays of some recent finds in the National Museum of Athens. My son made some sketches, so we can compare them to things we find in Olympia. It might help us date them more accurately."

Dodo crossed her legs and grabbed her knee. "About that, tell me more, Reginald. I find archeology terribly fascinating. Who's leading the dig?" She leaned forward, eyes wide. Reginald looked anywhere but at her, which was behavior she was unused to.

"Uh, Sir Roger Banbury is the current head," said Mr. Goodweather. "Over from Cambridge. Never met the fellow before but read some of his stuff while I was at university."

Dodo had never heard of the man, which wasn't too surprising, and wanted to ask her mother if she knew of him, although academics were not Lady Guinevere's specialty.

Reginald was picking at his trousers.

"What about this murder, then?" Dodo asked, stirring her cocktail and keeping her eyes low.

"Frightful!" declared Mr. Goodweather, like an old woman. "We were grilled by the police this afternoon and they had the temerity to tell us we cannot leave tomorrow. Overstepping their bounds in my opinion. Time is money on a dig."

"But you must see that they need to stop us from scattering," Rupert chimed in, circling his glass.

"I do not!" Mr. Goodweather was becoming quite excited. "It's not as though we had anything to do with it."

"Well, you do by association. The poor woman's death occurred while we were visiting the Parthenon, and I understand that she recognized someone from our group. The police *have* to question us all."

Mr. Goodweather's face paled. "Are you sure? The detective did not tell me that, he just asked us to stay in the area until further notice."

"Absolutely!" replied Dodo. "*I* am the witness that saw her, both here at the hotel and up at the Acropolis. She was peering at someone in our group outside the hotel as we were leaving, though I didn't see who. It would follow that one of us killed her."

"Ouch!" The younger Goodweather had bitten the cuticle at the side of his thumb and pulled off a great piece of skin, causing it to bleed. He pulled out a less than clean handkerchief and wrapped it around the wound.

"Ah, that does explain things," said Mr. Goodweather. "Why didn't the detective tell us?"

Dodo smoothed her black locks. "Well, the police don't like to show all their cards. At the moment, they are gathering information about the group since we all seem to have had opportunity." She glanced at Rupert to hand off the conversation.

"Since they found the murder weapon, they will now be looking for motives."

"The weapon?" asked Reginald, looking up from his thumb and entering the conversation for the first time.

"It appears Vera Fenchurch was killed with a hatpin to the heart," said Dodo.

Reginald shrank into his chair.

"I am not in the habit of wearing hatpins," said Mr. Goodweather, with a cross between a smile and a snarl.

"That may be," said Dodo. "But any of us could have found one on the floor or pinched one from someone. It seems to have been a murder of impulse rather than premeditation. The murderer would have used anything that came to hand."

"You seem to know a lot about all this," he said, by way of accusation.

"Lady Dorothea is a bit of a sleuth," explained Rupert, in an apparent effort to diffuse the thorny situation. "She is known to Sir Matthew Cusworth, head of Scotland Yard."

Jolly good tactic name dropping Sir Matthew!

Reginald stared at her while chewing the inside of his mouth. He really was a creepy little fellow.

Mr. Goodweather's shoulders relaxed. "Well, I never! That is unexpected for an earl's daughter."

"I find it keeps me interesting," retorted Dodo. "I am helping the police here, as a matter of fact."

Mr. Goodweather's shoulders tensed again.

"What if *you* are the killer?" said Reginald, his voice like an out of tune cello.

Dodo swiveled her body toward him, giving him the full force of her classic smile. He pushed up his glasses.

"It would be a jolly good method of remaining above suspicion," she said. "Detective Theodorou will no doubt keep that in mind."

"Did you know the Cartwrights have disappeared?" asked Rupert.

It was clear from the surprise on Mr. Goodweather's face that he did not. "Well, it's them then," he declared. "Only guilty people disappear after a murder."

"It is the behavior of the guilty to disappear, I agree," said Dodo. If the Goodweathers thought someone else was already on the hook for the murder, they might loosen up and reveal something useful. "Did you talk to them much?"

"Miss Cartwright didn't like me," said Reginald.

"What makes you say that?" she asked.

"I was playing tennis and my ball flew over the fence near her at the pool. I called her name and she ignored me."

Because she was not used to her assumed name.

"Did *you* happen to talk to them?" she asked his father.

"Not really. Not a real conversation, just small talk and no one can get to know anyone that way. And she was drunk that first night and went to bed early, if you remember."

"What about the Penhollands?" asked Rupert. "Have you got to know them?"

"Now, there is a lovely couple," Mr. Goodweather replied. "Had a smashing talk with them about the pyramids. That's where they're going next. They really appreciated my expertise."

"I'm sure they did," Dodo commented. "But it is my understanding that since we have all been delayed, Mrs. Penholland is very sore about it."

Mr. Goodweather clasped his hands around his knees. "I imagine so. We are! This was just supposed to be a short stop on the way to Olympia."

"Will a delay upset your schedule very much?" she asked.

"Not really," he said, hailing a waiter. "We can join anytime, it's just rather annoying. Port please," he said to the young man in black. "Reginald?"

"No thanks," replied his son.

"Where did you go to university?" Rupert asked Mr. Goodweather.

"Uh, well, my parents were a bit short on cash, so I went to Durham." His eyes darted back and forth at an alarming rate.

"Really?" remarked Rupert. "Does Durham have a good archeology department?"

"Oh, indeed. Thriving!" He stood. "Well, this has been lovely, but we must get to bed. Come Reginald."

"But your drink…" said Dodo.

"I shall take it to my room. Goodnight!"

The handkerchief around Reginald's thumb was pink with blood. He removed the cloth and stuck the thumb in his mouth giving Dodo the impression of an enormous baby.

Rupert and Dodo remained quiet until they were both out of earshot.

"What a load of poppycock!" declared Rupert. "Everyone knows Durham has an archaeology department, but I would bet my hat that he has never stepped foot on their campus by the speed at which he left. He didn't want to answer any more questions."

"They did leave rather abruptly," she agreed.

"And I know one shouldn't judge a book by its cover, but that Reginald is downright sinister."

"He is, but he seems more the type to poison someone than stab them," she responded.

Rupert slung the rest of the tumbler down his throat and smacked his lips. "Do you really think they are going on a dig?"

"No. That whole song and dance about Sir Roger Banbury being the head of the dig seems one detail too many. I need to check with Mummy if such a person exists." She tapped her mouth staring in the direction the Goodweathers had just walked. "I'd like to do some digging of my own."

"The discovery of the weapon and the flight of the Cartwrights distracted me from finding an expert at a local museum. We should try to do that soon," said Rupert.

They stood to leave and Dodo noticed something on the chair Mr. Goodweather had vacated. Reaching down, she saw that it was a crumpled piece of paper. It must have fallen out when he left a tip. Her heart picked up speed as she unfolded it.

Still no luck STOP Need payment STOP Do not return

It appeared to be the telegram that had upset him that first night. *Curious.*

She showed it to Rupert.

"Odd but not damning," he stated. "And it is rather vague."

Rupert was right, but she popped the telegram into her clutch. It might prove useful later.

They found Dodo's parents and Didi at the rooftop bar enjoying the scenery.

"Did you have dinner here?" Dodo asked.

"Yes, got in before the crowd, thankfully," said Dodo's mother. "Where did you two go?"

"We ate in the bar downstairs." She had warned Rupert that her mother did not like to talk about anything sordid. "We chatted with the Goodweathers."

"What a funny chap that son is!" remarked her mother. "Wouldn't say boo to a goose."

"Attached to his father at the hip," agreed Rupert.

"The way he looks at me makes me uneasy," piped in Didi.

"Mummy, do you know a Sir Roger Banbury? He may have something to do with archaeology."

Her mother tapped her glass. "Banbury...Banbury... Can't say that I do. Why?"

"It's not important. Someone mentioned the man in passing, and I wondered if you knew him."

"Is he married?" asked Guinevere. "What's his wife's name?"

Dodo shrugged. "I don't know." It wasn't hard evidence but if her mother did not know him it might indicate that Mr. Goodweather had fabricated the fellow. Where was *Burke's Peerage* when you needed one? She decided Rupert was right. It was time to visit a local museum to find out more about Olympia.

"Shall we play cards?" said Didi. "I can ask for some at the desk."

"Oh, yes," said her mother. "That will be fun. I find cards tell me a lot about a person." She smiled at Rupert. "Don't you?"

"You mean you find out who is a cheater," he said with a laugh. "My dear departed granny was the worst. She would sit on aces until she needed one."

Didi returned with a pack and they chose a simple game that did not require an even number. After several rounds it became evident that Rupert was something of an expert.

"You play a lot of cards at boarding school," he said as he shuffled like a professional.

While he was dealing at lightning speed, they were interrupted by a glowing Detective Theodorou.

"My dear Theodorou," said her father as if he and the rumpled policeman were old friends. "What can we do for you?"

"It is I who have news for you," he declared, raising his hands. "We have found the Cartwrights!"

"Were they missing?" asked Lady Guinevere.

"Briefly, Mummy," explained Dodo. "Where were they?"

"They had got as far as the border but had to change trains and were stopped by a station master who recognized them from the description we telegraphed to every major port and station. They're on their way back with a police escort, as we speak."

"That should be an interesting conversation," said Rupert.

The detective clicked his heels. "I thought you would like to know. Have a good evening."

Dodo jumped up to follow him. "I hear you interviewed the Goodweathers. Did you find out anything interesting?"

"Not really. They saw nothing and know nothing and since the only piece of circumstantial evidence I have on them is that they were in the location—as was everyone else—they are not on the top of my list of suspects." He turned to leave.

Too bad!

"I had a chat with them today," she said. He turned back to her. "I need to do more research on the subject, but I have suspicions that they are not going to Olympia for a dig at all. I'm going to a museum tomorrow to do my own research on the dig to see if their story holds water."

The detective raised his eyebrows. "Really? What makes you suspicious?"

"Rupert and I asked Mr. Goodweather where he went to university, and he said Durham. Apparently, it is well known that they have an archaeological school, but when pressed for more information he left abruptly."

The detective's frown slid to the left in skepticism. "That is not much to go on, m'lady. I have a bird in the hand."

"That is true but when coupled with the fact that they may not be going to the dig as they said—"

The detective held up his palm. "This is all speculation."

"Would *you* be willing to look up who is heading the dig?" she asked.

The detective shook his head. "I shall be busy grilling the Cartwrights."

"Then, could you tell me where I might go to investigate the dig details myself?" She cast a half smile at him and he sighed in resignation.

"Here." He took out his shabby notebook and scribbled something on it. "This man should have the information you need." He ripped out the page and handed it to her.

"You really believe the Cartwrights murdered Vera?" she asked, turning to leave.

"I am not sure, but they ran from the scene which is much more suspicious than your scenario. I must use my limited time with the more likely leads." He lifted his hat. "Good evening."

"I understand. I shall let you know if I find out anything interesting. Thank you, Detective Theodorou."

She placed the paper in her clutch purse and went back to find her family who were ready for the next round of the game. She thought about what the detective had said but her gut was still telling her that the Cartwright's secret was nothing to do with the death of the old lady.

Her money was now on the Goodweathers.

Chapter 14

The National Archaeological Museum of Athens was a beautiful pink building with white columns. On the roof of the entrance were several statues and the country's flag. The note the detective had given Dodo had not only the address but the name of the docent. A stale ticket desk faced Rupert and Dodo as they entered, and Dodo approached the ticket clerk.

"Good morning," she said. "I should like to speak to this person."

The quizzical look on the young man's face was evidence that he did not understand English but on seeing the name handwritten on the paper, he nodded. He pointed to the ticket price and they paid, then were led through the museum to a musty office with a tremendous view. A middle-aged man greeted them and indicated that they should sit, then formed a pyramid with his hands.

"Do you speak English?" Dodo asked.

"I was educated at Oxford," he explained in a voice almost devoid of accent. "Tell me, what can I do for you today?"

"My name is lady Dorothea Dorchester and this is Mr. Rupert Danforth." Rupert leaned across the desk to shake his hand. "I am interested in the archaeological dig at Olympia," she continued.

"Are you?" he said with intrigue.

"We may take a detour to visit if you think it worth our while."

His face shone with pride. "Oh, it is certainly worth your time, Lady Dorothea. Few sites provide as much view into the ancient past as that one." He went on to talk about the ruins of the venue of the first Olympic games, the exciting finds and the difficulty of removing several yards of soil and vegetation that covered the site.

"Isn't there an English chap leading the present dig?" asked Rupert.

"Present dig?" said the docent in surprise. "All active work stopped several months ago due to a lack of funding. Not since the departure of Ernst Curtius, have we been able to dedicate enough resources to this jewel. We are constantly lobbying for international funds to begin again. For Olympia is not just a gem in the mind of we Grecians, it is surely a precious monument for the whole world."

Dodo and Rupert stared at each other. Her memory about the article she had read had been correct.

"To be clear," said Rupert. "If someone wanted to join a dig today, they would not find such an opportunity at Olympia."

"That is correct. The nearest dig is sixty miles from there. But if you are interested in getting your hands dirty in such a project, I can steer you in the right direction." He pulled open a drawer and fiddled with some papers pulling one up and handing it over to Dodo. "Here is the information, if you are determined to see a dig in action."

Dodo felt her face fill with embarrassment. "I am sure it would be terribly exciting, but our interest is purely as tourists."

"Ah, well. It never hurts to try," he replied, genially.

They took their leave.

Outside the museum, Dodo could not contain herself.

"I *knew* the Goodweathers were lying," she exclaimed. "I just didn't have anything to back up my intuition."

"Now you do," said Rupert, placing an arm around her shoulder and kissing her on the nose.

"But this new information brings up another question. Why?" The museum was not far from the police station, their next port of call, and they started their walk along the bright, uneven sidewalks. "I think I shall have to send another telegram to David. See if he can dredge up anything." She stopped and Rupert stumbled. "But they could be using a false name too."

"I doubt they are the kind that would know how to get fake papers," said Rupert.

"True, true. C'mon, let's go!"

After a detour to the post office to send the telegram, they appeared at the police station. The desk clerk recognized them, asked them to wait, then returned with a smile and pointed down the hall to the detective's unassuming door.

"Good morning," said Theodorou looking even worse than he had the day before. His five o' clock shadow had evolved into a full-fledged beard. "What can I do for you?"

"They were lying," blurted out Dodo, dropping into one of the unsteady chairs.

"The Cartwrights? I think we have established that," he said, leaning back in his seat, hands behind his ruffled head.

"No! The Goodweathers."

The detectives heavy head fell to his chest. "More suspects?" He groaned. "Alright, tell me what you know." Three tiny, empty cups lined his desk.

Between the two of them, they told the tired detective everything they had learned at the museum.

He pointed a pencil at Dodo. "You were right."

"That's very decent of you to say so," she said with satisfaction. "So, the question is, if they are not in Greece to go on an archaeological dig, why are they here? And why the need to keep it a secret?" she asked.

The detective let his head fall into his hands. "I am beginning to believe your whole group had a hand in the murder."

"I know you are overworked, detective. But we are happy to help. I have already sent another telegram to England to see if I can sniff out any scandals concerning the Goodweathers," she explained. "I'll let you know what I find out."

"Are the Cartwrights back yet?" Rupert asked.

"Got here at five o'clock this morning." He leaned his greasy face on a large fist. "I am never going to get any rest until this case is closed."

"What did they say?" asked Dodo, trying to decide if asking to see them would be pushing her luck.

"Not much. I've put them in different cells, of course, but Mr. Cartwright or whatever his name is, has asked for a lawyer, which complicated things. I let him place a call to the British Consulate. And the woman, Phinella, is a bundle of nerves, crying and wailing. I would be wasting my time trying to get them to talk right now."

Dodo pursed her lips. "Do you allow visitors, by any chance?"

The detective squeezed a weary eye. "Yeees," he said slowly.

"While you are awaiting Mr. Cartwright's legal counsel, I can go in as a sympathizer. You know, woman to woman kind of thing. They don't need to know I'm aware of their subterfuge. I'll say I heard about the hunt and their arrest etc, etc…"

The detective gripped his mouth as he considered her proposition. "Couldn't hurt, I suppose."

"You would need to stay here," she said to Rupert, laying a hand on his chest. "Phinella will clam up if a man is present, but I think I can get her to talk if it's just me."

"In that case, I'll head back to the hotel and wait for you there," he said. "Will that be alright?"

"Absolutely!" She gave him a peck on the cheek and let the detective lead her to the cells.

If she really were interested in antiquities, she was now seeing one. It appeared that the ramshackle police station had been built over an ancient building. The walls were of raw limestone with holes bored into them at odd intervals. A slight shimmer gave the impression the walls were sweating in the dim light from single bulbs hanging along the eerie corridors.

The detective stopped in front of an iron and wood door with a huge lock. He removed an old-fashioned set of keys that would have looked at home on a Victorian housekeeper's belt and placed an impossibly large key into the giant keyhole. It turned with a scraping sound and he pushed the heavy door open. A short passage opened into a room containing four depressing, dark cells.

"I'll say I'm taking Mr. Cartwright up for questioning," Theodorou whispered. "You stand in the shadow just there until we are gone so he doesn't see you. I'll give you fifteen minutes."

Dodo obediently stepped into the shadows as he handled the keys and found a smaller one. "Time for a little chat," he said through the bars.

"Is my lawyer here yet?" barked Malcom. His voice was almost unrecognizable.

"He's on his way, no doubt," said the detective. "Aren't you ready for some food and light?"

"What about Phinella?" he said, his tone gruff.

"One at a time," Theodorou replied.

The lock turned and Malcolm flew out, rushing to the cell next door and gripping the bars with white knuckles. "I'll be back soon darling. I won't say anything."

The only reply was a moaning wail.

The detective pulled Malcolm's hands from the bars and pushed him toward the large door which shut with an ominous thud.

Dodo moved toward the cell, her shoes making a crisp smacking sound on the hard floor.

"Who's there?" cried a pitiful voice.

Dodo moved into the murky light cast by the lightbulb. "It's me. Lady Dorothea."

"What are *you* doing here?" said Phinella, as she approached the bars. "Can you believe this?"

"I know! I heard that you had been arrested, and I just *had* to come and see you," Dodo said. "I cannot imagine how terrible this must be for you."

A sad toddler could not have looked more pathetic. "We are being treated like common criminals," Phinella groaned. "They think we had something to do with the murder of that poor woman at the Acropolis."

"Why on *earth* would they think that?" cried Dodo, using her best amateur dramatics voice.

"They said it was because we left." She tucked her disheveled, red curls behind her ear. "We just wanted to do some more traveling," she whimpered.

It was telling that even in these dire circumstances Phinella was still maintaining the ruse. Perhaps they *were* spies, trained to maintain their cover at all costs. But her current misery didn't align with that line of reasoning.

"They *did* tell everyone not to leave," Dodo pointed out. "So it looked suspicious when you disappeared."

"I told Malcolm it would make us look guilty, but he said it was for the best."

"For the best? I don't understand," said Dodo.

Phinella took a while to answer. "I mean, we only have a limited time and there is so much still to see."

Dodo was getting tired of the lies and decided to push a little to get the ball rolling toward their fake identities.

"How do you explain the hatpin?"

With confused eyes, Phinella asked, "Hatpin? I don't know what you mean."

"Didn't Detective Theodorou tell you? Vera Fenchurch was killed with a hatpin." She paused for effect. "It was found under your mattress."

Phinella's hands flew to her mouth, panicked eyes round as plates.

"What? Lady Dorothea, you have to believe me! I didn't even know that was the murder weapon until you told me. We did not kill that woman!"

"I want to believe you," said Dodo. "But your disappearance coupled with finding the hatpin in your room are things the police cannot ignore. You must see that."

Phinella sank to her knees, face in her hands. An unnecessary performance if she was a hardened spy. Dodo waited.

"Here," Dodo finally said, holding a crisp white handkerchief through the bars.

With tear filled, red-rimmed eyes, Phinella reached up a hand to take it. Her wrenching heartache appeared genuine, and Dodo decided to adjust her pre-conceptions and treat Phinella as if what she said was true. "I don't believe you did it."

Phinella's head snapped up. "You don't?"

"No, but there are too many unanswered questions, and the police will pin this on whoever the evidence points to. Frankly, Theodorou is understaffed and wants a speedy outcome to this case. Do you really want to take your chances with a foreign jury?"

Phinella blinked in response, pushing tears down her miserable cheeks. Now Dodo was losing patience. She had to get the girl to see that stubborn silence could hang her.

"Unanswered questions, like, who you really are?" she said.

The imprisoned girl's eyes dropped to the floor. "I don't know what you mean?" she said, the hand holding the handkerchief trembling.

Time was running out. "If you continue to lie, I cannot help you," replied Dodo. "The police found a picture that had dropped behind the nightstand in your hotel room. It showed you and your *brother* in a compromising embrace."

A chewed lip indicated that Phinella might be on the verge of confessing something. Dodo just had to push her over the edge.

"He's not your brother, is he?" she asked.

Phinella shook her head.

Finally! "Did you run away for fear of being condemned for traveling with a man who is not your husband? Is all this deception about preserving a sense of morality?"

Phinella nodded.

"That wasn't so hard, was it? I'm sure if you tell Theodorou this, he will understand and agree that fear of discovery would be reason enough to flee."

The girl remained mute.

"That is a reason *I* can get behind," continued Dodo. "High class hotels like that tend to frown on such behavior. If it was revealed, you may have been asked to leave under a cloud and a girl has to think of her reputation. I understand completely."

The young woman wiped her fearful eyes and runny nose. "You are not shocked?"

"Shocked? A little, but I do not think such conduct is wise. If Malcolm should leave you, your chances at a happy life in the future are severely hindered." She drew a finger across her forehead. "Even if you are using false names."

"The police know about that? How?" gasped Phinella.

"In your haste you left clothes hanging in the wardrobe. They have laundry labels."

"Ah," said Phinella in a defeated tone. "We thought we were so careful."

"It's often the little, forgotten details that undo criminals in the end."

"But we are *not* criminals, Lady Dorothea!"

"Then you must defend yourself," cried Dodo. "Knowing your real name would help. Can't you give it to me? If you are to have any chance at avoiding prosecution it is the least you can do."

"Fanny Lyman," she murmured.

That matched the initials. "Alright. That is progress. And is that the only reason you bolted?"

"Yes. When you told us at lunch that the police said we could not leave, I knew it was only a matter of time until they found out we weren't who we said we were and then everything would fall apart."

"And you have fake passports in the name of Cartwright. Those are not easy to get."

She raised doleful eyes. "M…Malcolm took care of all of that."

"Such draconian measures," said Dodo. "Does his family not approve of you?"

Her shoulders dropped. "You could say that," she replied. "We just wanted to be together and thought we would be safe this far from home. Then that woman was killed and everything we had worked for was put in peril. We panicked and ran. We hoped we could get back to France and lay low. Re-emerge as ourselves in a month or two when the heat was off and the murder solved. But the station master recognized us and wouldn't let us get on the connecting train. I almost died of fear." She looked behind her at the sorry cell. "And now I'm in jail. It is like a terrible nightmare. We just wanted a nice h—holiday together."

The coil of doubt was beginning to unwind in Dodo's head.

"I will talk to Detective Theodorou. He can look into your claims and if they are proved to be true it will help your defense. Presumably you have some identification that proves you are who you say you are."

A door slammed and the girl shut down again. Strain reappeared around her eyes.

"If you won't confide in me, I cannot help." Dodo moved toward the door.

"Wait."

Dodo turned back and crunched across the dirty floor. "Yes?"

"I didn't even know that a hatpin had been used to kill that woman. And if I had killed her, why would I leave it to be found by the police. I believe someone is trying to frame us."

This, of course, was the line of reasoning Dodo had presented to the detective herself. "If it eases your mind, that is something the detective is considering." She turned to leave.

"Lady Dorothea, I do not want you to think ill of me."

"I am not here to judge," assured Dodo. "I want to try to help. Goodbye."

Theodorou had left the heavy, wooden door unlocked. As Dodo closed it behind her she heard a wretched sob.

Chapter 15

Though having trouble staying awake, Detective Theodorou was all ears when Dodo recounted her conversation with Phinella, or Fanny. However, Dodo felt compelled to admit that she still sensed the girl was holding out on her.

The detective waved a paper. "And I have news for you. I have just received a telegram from England with details about the murder victim."

"Anything of interest there?" she asked.

He handed her the page.

Vera Millicent Fenchurch STOP Born 1854 Hampshire STOP Single STOP Nanny to McTavish family of Aberdeen, Radford Family of Kent STOP retired STOP

"Not much to go on but I shall ask my mother if she has heard of either family. She's often more efficient than *Burke's*."

"*Burke's*?" he said, a furrow of lines on his forehead. "I do not know this name."

"It's a publication listing the genealogies of the peers of England," Dodo explained. "But Mummy has so many friends and acquaintances that she often knows people that come up in my investigations. She's really rather marvelous."

"Yes," replied the detective, his eyes misting.

Dodo cleared her throat.

"I would be most obliged," he replied, repositioning his crooked tie.

"I don't suppose you've heard anything from the British intelligence division about the so-called Cartwrights?"

He shook his head. "Do you still think they are spies?"

"Phinella's, or rather Fanny's, behavior just now, does not lend itself to that conclusion. But one never knows.

Best to have the proper verification." She looked around the sparse room. There were no pictures or ornamentation of any kind. It was rather too like the cells she had just left. "Are you going to question the Goodweathers again? You need to confront them with the details about Olympia I discovered."

"I suppose I must," he complained.

"I'll let you know what I find out, from Mummy, if anything," she said as she left the room.

Checking in at the hotel desk, Dodo was delighted to be handed another telegram from David. She ripped it open.

Checked archived newspapers STOP younger Goodweather accused of manhandling young girl five years ago Kent STOP father lost reputation and job defending son STOP never prosecuted STOP left country STOP you owe me STOP

She tapped her wrist with the paper. *Well, well, well!*

Kent! Didn't Theodorou just mention Kent? Could Reginald have caused a scandal with a girl in Vera Fenchurch's charge? If so, it could have been *him* she recognized. And if the Goodweathers had come abroad to get away from tattling tongues only to come face to face with one, they may have snapped. She clapped her hands. She was now in possession of means, opportunity, *and* motive for the father and son. Whatever the Cartwrights were guilty of, she was more convinced than ever that it was not the murder of Vera Fenchurch.

She called Theodorou and told him about her telegram before he interviewed the pair. He received the news with a tired groan.

Mind on the things she had just learned, Dodo turned to go up to her room and bumped straight into Mrs. 'Gus' Penholland.

"I do beg your pardon!" Dodo cried.

'Gus was quite undone. "You should really watch where you are going, Lady Dorothea," she blurted out, adjusting her hat with wild eyes.

"Yes, I'm terribly sorry," she repeated. "I just got some fascinating news from home and was not paying attention."

"Oh?" 'Gus's face reflected both disdain and curiosity. A better stage villain could never be found.

Although what Dodo had learned implicated the Goodweathers, there was something about this woman she truly disliked. And a conscientious investigator left no corner unswept. However, she was not about to divulge the fresh information from England on this unworthy specimen. She would satisfy that eager gleam in 'Gus's eye with news she was bound to find out soon anyway.

"The Cartwrights have been apprehended. They are in the cells at the police station," Dodo told her.

'Gus's witch-like mouth dropped open. "Ha! I knew there was something off about that pair," she spat. "Perhaps we will be allowed to leave now that they have the murderers under lock and key."

"You believe them to be the guilty party?"

"Certainly. The murder weapon was found under their mattress and they absconded. What more could the detective ask for? A confession?"

"How did you know about the hatpin?" asked Dodo.

A tinge of color breathed life into her leather-like skin. "It's all over the hotel," 'Gus explained. "Gossip like that, spreads like wildfire."

"Detective Theodorou is not as convinced by the hatpin as you appear to be," said Dodo. "Inconsistent behavior, I believe is the proper term for it."

"Inconsistent what?" spluttered 'Gus.

"You see, they were very deliberate in what they took when they left, which is not consistent with leaving the murder weapon under the mattress for the police to find. No matter how cold the killer, they would not be able to forget the very object they committed the murder with. It would haunt them. So, if they were the culprits, they would either have disposed of it, which would have been quite easy in the large hotel bins by the kitchens or down a drain or some such, or placed it in their luggage or in a hat, to throw away later in a random place where it would never be found. One hatpin is much like another and it would be hard to prove that any particular pin had been the actual weapon. In short, they would have been idiots to leave it."

'Gus narrowed her beady, hooded eyes. "Well, they were not the brightest pair. Perhaps they just forgot in their panic to leave."

It was difficult to overturn people's biases. "Such a thing is more than unlikely," Dodo explained. "Anyway, it doesn't matter what *we* think, it's what the *detective* thinks that matters, and he is not convinced."

'Gus snarled, pushing out her flappy bottom lip. "I have to go! Good day, Lady Dorothea."

Dodo watched her make an abrupt about turn and depart for the elevators, her thin legs taking her with surprising speed.

Something had spooked her.

Floating in the massive swimming pool with Rupert was a well-deserved rest. The luxurious pool was a dazzling, sky blue with the Parthenon as a backdrop. White cabanas with navy and white padded cushions, stretched out on both sides like bodyguards. A giant, white pergola sat proudly at the top deck of the pool, and bronzed pool boys stood ready to fulfill your every whim. The water was warm, and Rupert held her hand as they lay face up to the sun. She had told him everything, even about bumping into 'Gus in the lobby. They were currently making up ridiculous scenarios to explain her odd behavior.

"She had come down to get wart ointment for Mr. Penholland and realized he was still upstairs, barefoot, awaiting her return," said Rupert.

Dodo giggled. "How about, she was securing a special pillow to relieve piles and did not want me to see the concierge bring the item."

"Dodo you have a wicked mind," he said, holding his belly.

He rolled over onto his front and ran a wet finger along her collarbone.

"Try this," he said. " 'Gus placed the hatpin in the Cartwright's room to remove suspicion from herself and was spooked to hear that Theodorou believed it was planted."

Dodo slapped the water sending a shower of droplets onto his face.

"Dodo! I was joking! What makes you think it was her? Everything is pointing to the Goodweathers or the Cartwrights or whatever their real names are."

"How did 'Gus know the hatpin was under the mattress? Theodorou has gone to pains *not* to release that detail and no one but us was there when he came into the bar brandishing the thing. She said she heard the rumor around the hotel, but that detail was not made public— the staff would not have known."

"Perhaps he mentioned it during their interview?"

Fiddlesticks! It had seemed like a brilliant burst of genius a minute ago. She would need to ask the detective about it.

She sighed. "Maybe. I was trying to think laterally. But you didn't see her face, Rupert. It was like she had received news that a favorite aunt had died. I am sure she hustled back upstairs to tell her husband. But why?"

"Because she is a gossipy old biddy who lives for drama and to sew malicious rumor abroad."

Dodo flipped over. "You're probably right."

She hefted herself out of the pool and reached for a towel, blotting her navy, white polka dot bathing costume. She took off her bathing cap and slung it on the lounger, shaking her jet-black hair out as her mother entered the pool deck.

"Darling!" waved Lady Guinevere.

"Come and join us," Dodo replied. There's plenty of room."

Her mother was covered head to toe, as usual, and took the lounger next to Dodo's. "Your father is taking a nap, and I thought I would enjoy being out by the pool."

"It is rather serendipitous as I have a question for you." She wrapped herself in the fluffy towel and positioned herself on the lounger. "Have you ever heard of either the McTavishes of Aberdeen or the Radfords of Kent?"

Lady Guinevere chewed her cheek as she considered. "Let me think…McTavish…" She shot a hand in the air. "Cynthia Melrose married a McTavish back in 1897. Gosh, I haven't thought of her for ages. We came out together, you know. Lovely girl, we got on like a house on fire. I think she was from Nottingham. I stayed at her house once before I married. Yes. Now, what was her husband's name. It was very Scottish I remember. Hamish? Callum?" Her hand shot up again. "Angus. Angus McTavish. It's almost comical." She looked at Dodo with triumph.

"Did they have children?"

Rupert lifted himself over the edge of the pool, his fine physique glistening in the Greek sun and Dodo temporarily lost her train of thought.

"A boy and a girl. No, wait! Two boys and a girl…but one of the boys died."

This brought Dodo back. "How awful. How did he die?"

"I believe he drowned or fell. It was terrible. I sent a note of condolence."

This was sad but seemingly irrelevant information.

"What was the other family?" her mother asked, checking her lipstick in a compact mirror.

"Radford of Kent," Dodo replied with bated breath.

"Margaret Radford? Heavens, yes! Known her forever though I see less of her now than I used to. She's a little older than me. She had a son who took over the estate when her husband died. I rather think there was some kind of scandal there a few years ago."

Dodo forced herself to remain calm. Drawing information out of her mother could be tricky. If she caught a whiff of salaciousness or murder, she would shut up tight like a Venus flytrap.

"Who did *he* marry?" Dodo asked.

"Some girl Margaret didn't like. Edith or something. I remember she was rude to poor Margaret on the wedding day and spoilt the whole thing for her, but she had to pretend her feelings weren't hurt. She thought the girl might be the kind to withhold access to the grandchildren if crossed. You know the type."

"How dreadful," responded Dodo pulling the damp towel off and flinging it on the ground.

"It was the daughter-in-law that made all the fuss, if I remember right," murmured her mother.

"Now you've lost me," lied Dodo, hoping her mother would recall more and fill in the details.

"The scandal! The daughter-in-law accused someone of messing with her daughter, Margaret's granddaughter. Frightful business!"

Careful now.

"Not sure I blame her if the mother was protecting her children," said Dodo in an even tone.

"Margaret thought Edith was overreacting and so did the nanny, but Edith would have none of it and sent all the guests packing. Caused quite a stir at the time."

"I don't suppose you remember who she accused?" Dodo crossed her fingers.

Lady Guinevere frowned. "You know I hate nastiness in any form. I didn't ask."

"How long ago would that have been?" asked Dodo.

Her mother looked up at the sky twisting her lips. "Not more than five years ago."

Five years! This fell around the same time as the incident David spoke of. Things were not looking good for peculiar Reginald.

Chapter 16

Dodo had dressed simply for dinner in a drop-waist, scarlet dress with matching headband and a black wrap.

"Red is definitely your color," said Rupert, eating her up with his eyes. He slung an arm around her shoulders and kissed her just below the ear. He was clean and natural as a tropical waterfall, and she rewarded his affection with a lingering kiss.

Tonight, they were eating dinner with her parents on the middle floor. Their sailing trip had now been delayed two days. Dodo was itching to get going and show Rupert the idyllic Greek islands surrounded by azure water and white sand but there were still too many loose ends in the case, and her mind was constantly working on the problem.

Didi had managed to get her photos developed and as they were waiting for their food, they looked through them. Most of the shots were of flower-filled courtyards and ruins as she had said, but several of them had caught Dodo and Rupert, a couple good enough that Dodo wanted her own copy to put in a frame. So far, only a few had even part of Phinella's face, or Fanny as she now knew her to be, or Malcolm. Not that it really mattered since they were already in custody.

Dodo was still convinced they were not the killers, which logically meant one of the other couples was guilty. She hoped that the information about the family in Kent her mother had divulged, and the fact that there was no Olympia dig, was enough to convince the detective, who was still solely focused on the Cartwrights.

As she flicked through the pictures, she stopped on the second to last. It was a picture of Fanny and Malcolm Cartwright looking off into the distance, totally unaware that Didi had caught them on film. She tried to recast them as lovers rather than brother and sister. First impressions were hard to erase at the best of times.

Dodo thought back to the photograph she had found in their room to compare it to this. Fanny wore her pale, auburn hair rolled up at the back and in Marlene waves on the sides. Had she worn it like that in the other picture? She squeezed her eyes shut trying to conjure up a clearer image of the kiss. She could envision the side waves, but she had the nagging feeling there was something in that photograph that was missing here. It was tickling the edge of her brain.

"Will you excuse me?" she said, rising and replacing the wrap around her shoulders. "I need the little girl's room." No need to upset her mother.

Rupert looked quizzical and she hoped she communicated that she would be back in a minute and there was no cause for alarm.

She hurried over to the elevator and down to the front lobby.

"I wonder if I might be allowed to use your phone again," she asked the young man at the desk.

"Of course," he replied and gestured for her to go behind the desk into the small office with the frosted glass door.

"Athens police station."

The operator said something back in Greek that she hoped meant yes.

A gruff, unintelligible voice picked up the phone speaking Greek.

"Theodorou?" she asked.

More unidentifiable language and then the phone was picked up again.

"Theodorou." He sounded like a man who was in dire need of sleep and a good homecooked meal.

"I am sorry to bother you, detective, but I wonder if you have access to the picture I found of the Cartwright's kissing?"

"It's in my file. What are we looking for?"

"My sister took a photo of them on the day they disappeared, and I have been trying to compare the two shots in my mind. My memory is saying there was something in Miss Cartwright's hair in the picture you have, and I am hoping you can take a look for me."

She could hear papers shuffling. "Here it is."

"Can you look at her waves specifically. Is there something in her hair?"

"You mean like a decorative clip or something?" he asked.

"I suppose so."

"Nothing like that," he replied.

"Is there nothing on her hair?"

"There *is* a blurry object that looks like it is near her hair but not on it."

The hairs on Dodo's arms bristled.

"Yes! Look at that. Can you make out what it is?"

There was a moment of silence. "Let me get a magnifying lens," he said.

Dodo's toes were curled in anticipation as she heard a drawer open and some scraping.

"Well, I never!" declared the detective.

"What!" demanded Dodo, impatience drilling her head like a woodpecker.

"It's a heart. A tiny heart."

This was *not* what she had expected to hear. "A heart?" *A heart, a heart*. Then her brain fired in an explosion of understanding. "Confetti!"

"Lady Dorothea, you are a marvel," said the tired detective. "Now that you put a name to it, I can tell that it *is* confetti. There is part of another one visible on Mr. Cartwright's shoulder."

"So, this is not a picture of two clandestine lovers in an embrace," she blurted out. "It is a picture of two people who just got married!" Everything they had told her, and

123

everything she had assumed, now turned upside down again.

Theodorou grunted. "But why would they hide the fact that they are married? It is much better for a young lady's reputation to be known as a new bride."

"That is a good question and one you should ask them immediately, detective. They are still holding out on us and we need to know why. It could be key. I'll call you back after I have eaten. I think this might be pivotal to their defense," she declared.

Rupert raised his eyebrows as she took her seat next to him, letting the wrap fall to the back of the chair. He placed his hand on hers and tapped it with a finger.

"I'll tell you later," she whispered in his ear, her lip catching his lobe as she pulled away.

Though the food had arrived, everyone was still engrossed in looking at Didi's photos and Didi, her mother and father, were commenting on one in particular.

"This one is marvelous!" declared her mother, turning it around. It was the one Dodo liked, of the two of them near the market. Didi had managed to capture a splendid candid shot of her and Rupert gazing into each other's eyes with evident tenderness.

"I know! I want to put it in a frame. Can you get a copy?" she asked her sister.

"You can have that one," said Didi. "I have the negative."

Dodo took the picture and slipped it in her clutch bag as the waiters brought local fish for everyone.

With one eye on the clock, Dodo tucked in. The soft, white meat was aromatic, melting in her mouth. Although everyone was merry around her, the recent revelation about the so-called Cartwrights filled her thoughts so much that she could not join in. Her mind was on the interview currently underway at the police station.

Her mother laughed at something Didi said, bringing her back from her muddled thoughts and it reminded Dodo that she had been so wrapped up in the Cartwright drama, that she had completely forgotten to tell Theodorou about David's latest telegram and her mother's knowledge of the families for whom Vera Fenchurch had nannied. She wondered if she could sneak away to call him again without eating dessert.

As the plates were cleared, the head waiter came to their table.

"Tonight, is the breaking of the plates. You will enjoy? No?"

Her mother's face lit up like a child who has been told there is going to be a second Christmas Eve. "Oh yes! How wonderful! I think we have only done it once before." She looked around the table. "It is such fun!"

Dodo knew there would be no getting away now.

All the guests were driven to the end of the room, organized into a loose circle, and handed a plain white plate. Rupert looked at Dodo with curious incomprehension on his face.

"It's an ancient tradition linked to dispelling evil spirits," she explained. "Nowadays, they only do it for the tourists. Follow my lead."

A trio of musicians entered wearing the traditional, long, white shirt, white stockings and blue and gold waistcoat caught round the middle with a red sash. A red tasseled cap completed the costume. Each of them played traditional Greek music with a lute and as the head waiter clapped slowly and stamped his feet to the lilting rhythm of the sound, the air filled with an intoxicating charge.

The head waiter nodded to Dodo who yelled, "Opa!" and threw her plate to the ground amid cheers and applause.

Rupert's eyes widened with shock and a wry smile spread over his features.

"Your turn," she said to him as the rhythmic music built momentum.

He lifted the plate high above his head, crying, "Opa!" as the plate smashed to smithereens in the middle of the group of guests. Now he was beaming ear to ear.

"I can see the appeal," he said with a rumbling laugh that made her heart clench. "It's quite liberating!"

The Penhollands were both in the restaurant but only Mr. Penholland was in the circle. 'Gus was radiating disapproval from the other side of the room. When her husband's turn came, he thrust the plate to the floor with both hands and grinned in triumph, cheeks flaming as cheers from all those in the circle, filled the air.

Didi threw her plate good and hard while Lady Guinevere managed a little toss with one hand that produced only a chip on her plate. Lord Dorchester accidentally dropped his and it split in half at his feet. He shrugged.

When everyone had taken a turn, and a pile of plate shards were in the middle of the circle, everyone placed their arms on the shoulders of the person next to them to form an unending chain, and began the traditional Greek folkdance, bending low and moving to the right. For ten minutes, Dodo forgot about murder, confetti and fake passports and let herself surrender to the music and fun. Whooping and hollering, one of the waiters even leapt on a table and danced.

"I could do that every night!" declared Rupert as the musicians wandered away and they returned to their table. Waiters brought large brooms to sweep up the broken china.

"Me too, but I think they would run out of plates very quickly," she said with a laugh. "They just do it once a week."

"Makes sense but it is rather fun. Might try it out at one of my parties," Rupert declared.

"That would make a splash!" she agreed. "Wait! You throw parties?"

"I have been known to organize the odd bash. Not at the mews house, you understand. Much too small. I usually rent out a place once or twice a year."

"How marvelous and how have I never been invited to one?" she asked with a tilt of her head.

"That is an error I intend to rectify, henceforth," he said, cupping her chin with his hand and landing a gentle kiss on her lips. "Perhaps I can help with your twenty-first birthday bash?"

"Now, now," said her old-fashioned father. "Not in public, eh?"

Lady Guinevere slapped him on the arm. "Don't be silly, darling! Everyone enjoys seeing young love-birds kiss."

Lord Dorchester huffed into his mustache as they took their seats back at the table to finish dessert.

"That's put me in a festive mood," declared Didi, "and I don't want the night to end. What else shall we do tonight? I think there's dancing on the ground floor."

"What a grand idea," said their mother. "I'm feeling rather romantic after all that plate smashing. What do you say, Alfie?"

"Jolly good!" he replied.

"We'll join you in a bit," said Dodo. "We want to take a little stroll first." She took Rupert's arm and steered him to the elevator before the rest of the family could react. Once inside, she explained what she and Theodorou had discovered.

"That's why you were so quiet during dinner," he responded.

"Well, that and the divine fish," she said. "But now I'm dying to know how the interview went, and I realized that I forgot to tell him all the new things I have learned."

They made a beeline for the front desk and after asking to use the phone, entered the small office with only one chair. Rupert sat and pulled her onto his lap while she dialed the operator and was put through to the station.

"Tell me what happened with the Cartwrights," she said as soon as Theodorou picked up. She and Rupert sat head-to-head, the receiver between them.

"The consulate finally sent a lawyer—stuffed shirt, you know the type—and I got them both up here to meet with him. But before they could consult, I announced that I had reason to believe they were married. At first, they both sat in shocked silence and the lawyer asked if that was true. After whispering at length with the legal chap, Mr. Cartwright admitted to the fact and asked how I knew. I showed them the photo and pointed to the confetti. It was like a dam bursting after that."

"What do you mean?"

"Well, the lawyer is interested in proving their innocence to the murder, and he advised them that the truth would provide a compelling reason for their flight. Turns out we have a bit of a Romeo and Juliet story on our hands, minus the suicide. Mr. Malcolm Cartwright's real name is Matthew Longbourne—"

"Longbourne? Why is that familiar?" she asked.

"Because his family makes the most popular brand of toothpowder," explained the detective.

"Of course!" she cried.

"And Phinella Cartwright *was* actually Frances Longhurst but is now Mrs. Matthew Longbourne."

"Of Longhurst toothpaste?" Dodo asked, cogs and wheels turning in her head.

"Exactly! Like I said, the Capulets and the Montagues."

"I am impressed with your analogy detective."

"I'm not a complete ignoramus," he rebutted.

"Sorry, I didn't mean to suggest…anyway. The two children of deadly rivals meet and fall in love and know their families will not approve of their marriage, so they elope. Oh, my goodness! This is their *honeymoon*— and they got apprehended and thrown in jail!"

"Correct. They ran away to get married, having got themselves a couple of fake passports—"

"More than one?" interrupted Dodo. That would explain the other fake name Phinella had given her.

"They each had two in case they ran into trouble and needed a backup. They left England as husband and wife, disguised as brother and sister. That way, no one would question them sharing a room. They picked Greece as far enough away from England to avoid detection and maintained the brother-sister act in case being newlyweds caused people to make a fuss, which was the last thing they wanted. The plan was to lay low until things had blown over at home. They hoped that if they were gone long enough, their families would be so relieved they were alive it would soften the blow that they had married."

"And the murder jeopardized everything," filled in Dodo. "When I told them they wouldn't be able to leave Athens until the investigation was over, and that they would be interviewed, they got scared they would be unveiled and made a run for it."

"Exactly," said Theodorou.

Dodo and Rupert stared at each other in disbelief.

"Are you still holding them for the murder?" she asked.

"For the time being, since I cannot be one hundred percent sure that it wasn't *them* Miss Fenchurch recognized. They may have murdered her to keep their secret, though at this point I doubt it. But they had certainly gone to a lot of trouble to hide their real identities."

"True. But I think I can throw some more reasonable doubt on the case against them. In all the excitement about working out that the Cartwrights were actually married, I forgot to tell you that my mother knows both the families that Miss Fenchurch nannied for. She told me that the family in Scotland suffered a terrible misfortune when their young son died tragically many years ago. I don't know many other details and don't think it is relevant to this situation. But the second family, the Radfords, is much more applicable to this case. They had to send a male guest packing when the mother thought he had messed with her daughter. When mother told me this, I had just received a telegram from my friend in England that confirmed that Reginald Goodweather was accused of molesting someone's daughter. Both circumstances happened in Kent, and around the same time, though I cannot confirm it is the same family at present."

"Good grief!" moaned the detective. "I have more motives than a German opera!"

"Have you re-interviewed the Goodweathers yet?" she asked.

"They are due any minute. I asked them to come after dinner." She heard the chink of a cup. "The information you have gathered for me is invaluable, Lady Dorothea. Between that and the lie about the dig, the spotlight has been thrown on the Goodweathers and away from the Longbournes, as we now know them. But, may I remind you that I am a one-man show and I need to get my notes written before the Goodweathers arrive for questioning. I shall have to go." He hung up.

"You didn't tell him about 'Gus," said Rupert.

"The poor man is already overwhelmed," she said as she replaced the receiver. "I shall tell him that later. Who knows, the Goodweathers may confess!"

Chapter 17

After the call ended and they had taken a moment to discuss all the explosive revelations, Dodo and Rupert joined her parents for the dancing.

The intimate ballroom was softly lit with gas lamps, the floor a mosaic design in the Greek style, now covered with couples. A small band played soft jazz as a talented singer crooned into a microphone. She spied Didi on the sidelines, elbow on the table, stubborn chin glued to her palm and a sadness in her eyes. She would let her borrow Rupert.

Her parents were gliding skillfully across the floor. Her father was a big man, both tall and stocky, but he was surprisingly light on his feet. There was something remarkably comforting to the soul to see one's parents clearly dotty about each other and genuinely enjoying one another's company. So many of her friends' parents were locked in passionless marriages that had been arranged by their families twenty years before. The world had changed so much since those days.

"Hello," said Dodo to her sister. "Not enjoying yourself as a gooseberry?"

"Daddy has danced with me twice, but I miss Charlie terribly." Her pretty mouth shrugged.

"Of course, you do." Dodo tipped her head to her sister and raised her brows at Rupert.

"Oh, yes. Uh, would you care to dance, Didi?" he managed to say.

Her sister glanced at Dodo to check that she was alright with this arrangement.

"What a wonderful idea," said Dodo. "I shall rest my feet. Go! Go!" She flicked her hand toward the dance floor.

Rupert took Didi's arm and led her to the middle of the dancing couples. From a distance Dodo was able to admire his smooth moves and adroit footwork. He really was a prize in so many ways and she felt very fortunate. His golden hair was combed back from his animated, strong brow as he listened intently to Didi's conversation. His familiar profile evoked a sudden yearning for a pencil and paper. Could it be more perfect?

Her parents swung by Rupert and smiled like guardian angels, approving of the situation. As she had hoped they would, her parents and sister had welcomed Rupert in seamlessly. There had been no awkward first introductions, no pointed questions. He had been made an honorary part of the family on first sight, and she loved them for it.

She leaned back in her chair and hailed a waiter for a cocktail. While she awaited his return, she looked around the room to see if there was anyone else she recognized. Predictably, the Penhollands were absent and she realized with a pang that the other pairs were either in jail or at the police station for questioning. However, as her eyes traveled the room, she caught sight of Lizzie passing an arch. A glance at the time told her it was past Lizzie's bedtime. Was she meeting the handsome valet, Mr. Scott?

The die was cast. She had to snoop. It was in her nature. She couldn't help it.

Dodo walked slowly around the tables and through the arched doorway looking left and right. Following the direction Lizzie had taken, she saw a door to a patio lit with torches and slipped through.

Keeping to the shadows, she crept forward and stopped abruptly as she saw the silhouettes of two people standing close, looking out over the city at the Acropolis. She cursed that their backs were to her but knew Lizzie's outline like the back of her hand.

As if she had made the request herself, the young man turned to Lizzie and the light of a nearby torch lit his features. It was a sharp, angular, but pleasant face, with close-set dark eyes and a determined chin. By any standard he was an attractive young man, and Dodo felt delighted for her treasured maid.

As she stood watching, Lizzie turned to face Mr. Scott and he placed a hand on her shoulder, leaning forward. It was time to leave. Though Dodo was dying to know if they were kissing in the moonlight, she respected her maid's privacy and slipped back the way she had come, grinning like the proverbial Cheshire cat.

When she made it back to the table, her drink was waiting. She took a little sip as her family walked off the dance floor, and Rupert held out his hand to her. Her heart beat a little faster. He twirled her in a circle like a pro, catching her round the waist, and pulling her in so close she could feel his breath fan her forehead. Melting into his embrace, she let him guide her through the motions of the dance. There was a reason that dancing was a universal courting ritual. On the dance floor a level of intimacy was permitted that would be frowned upon elsewhere, and plenty of privacy for secret conversation or silent communication. Touch, so important in cultivating relationships, was not only allowed, it was encouraged.

She had been in relationships with many men in her time, but no one had turned her world on its head like Rupert. Not even the infamous Chief Inspector Blood. She was more and more sure she had found the one.

"So, what are you thinking?" he murmured into her ear.

"That you might be the best thing that ever happened to me." It was a bold statement but one she felt confident making.

He chuckled, and she could feel the vibration in her chest. "Then I am a step ahead of you," he whispered. "Because I *know* you are the best thing that has ever happened to me."

She looked up at him through her dark, long lashes, the words 'I love you' on the tip of her tongue. She wondered if he was thinking the same.

Cupping her hand around his firm shoulder, she leaned her face against his chest.

"It is obvious to me that the Cartwright's did not kill Vera Fenchurch."

She felt his body shake.

"What?"

He laughed out loud. "Is that your idea of romantic banter? You are the only girl I know who would puncture a tender moment with a statement about murder."

"It is part of my glittering appeal," she declared, with a chuckle.

"It is," he agreed.

"And you love me for that quirky quality."

"I do," he said into her hair.

Could this be the moment?

"You do what?" she asked.

"I do love you."

For the next few minutes, they kissed as they danced.

"I love you too," she said, her voice ragged.

The slow song ended, and they changed their grip as a faster number began. "Anyway, how can you be so sure about the Cartwrights?" he asked.

"You should have seen Phinella, well, Frances, in the jail cell. She was utterly undone. If they *had* committed murder, her genuine misery in jail is proof to me there is no way she would have summoned the composure necessary to go to lunch with us and act as if everything was normal. No. Their anxiety began the minute I said there would be an investigation and that none of us would be able to leave, not before. And she appeared genuinely shocked when I told her the murder weapon was a hatpin."

"Ok, you have convinced me," he murmured. "What about the Goodweathers?"

"That is a completely different kettle of fish," she said as they glided round the floor. "We know for a fact that they have lied about being here since there is no dig in Olympia.

If Reginald is the 'guest' that was asked to leave in Kent—a family for whom Vera Fenchurch nannied—we have a tremendously compelling motive. Dressed in the garb of an archeologist, with a hat and beard, Vera would have had trouble recognizing Reginald. To be certain before approaching him, she may have followed us. Human nature being what it is, she might have seen it as a perfect opportunity for blackmail."

"What about the hatpin under the Cartwright's bed? That would mean the Goodweathers put it there and I must say, they also seemed positively shocked that a hatpin was the murder weapon, that night in the bar."

She smirked. "Shocked or guilty? People who have committed a crime feel exposed, as if their guilt is written on their foreheads for all the world to see."

"But a hatpin is a curious weapon for a man, don't you think?"

"Is it? I lose hatpins regularly," she explained. "They slip out and you don't notice until there is a gust of wind or you get home. Clearly, given the circumstances, they would have had to act in haste to stamp out the threat before she could expose them. It could just as easily have been a heavy rock or a piece of metal bar. It probably glinted in the sunlight. But you see, it didn't really matter, they used what was around because it was so urgent."

"But wouldn't they have disposed of it up there?" he asked.

"Oh, Rupert! You're thinking like a murderer!" She kissed him. "Of course! They would have cleaned the hatpin and dropped it somewhere it would never be found. The one placed under the mattress was not the *actual* murder weapon, it was just a means to send suspicion elsewhere. Here's what I think happened. There was no reason to connect our group to a random murder so they thought they had got away with it scot-free. But then they were called in for initial questioning by Theodorou and told that I had seen the woman follow our group—remember, we only have their word that they did not know I had given a statement—they must have panicked. I'm guessing they stole a hatpin from the pool or somewhere and slipped it under the Cartwright's mattress when the room was being cleaned. But Theodorou did disclose that a hatpin could have been the murder weapon. That is the important fact."

"Dastardly." He grinned, dipping her to the floor then pulling her up so their lips were only a gnat's wing apart. A giggle began in the pit of her stomach and worked its way up through her throat.

"That is what murderers are," she finally said.

"So, you're letting old 'Gus off the hook?"

"I really want it to be her because she is so ghastly, and I feel sorry for her poor, hen-pecked husband. But the evidence *is* pointing to the Goodweathers."

The musicians stopped and announced that they were taking a short break. Rupert led her back to the table where she was surprised to see Mr. Penholland, enjoying a natter with her father.

"Hello, darling!" said Lord Dorchester. "Miles was just telling me that he used to live in Scotland."

Dodo started, then recovered herself and turned on a high wattage smile. "Whereabouts?" she asked, goose pimples breaking out on her arms.

"Here and there," he hedged. "I moved around quite a bit."

Non-committal. Was he hiding something?

"I have a favorite hunt up above Aberdeen," continued her father. "Friend of mine has a castle up there. Best deer hunting in the land in my opinion."

"I agree," said Mr. Penholland. "I've hunted all over Scotland in my time, before I married Augusta of course, and that *is* the best."

"How did you meet your wife?" Dodo asked casually, gripping the sides of her chair.

"It was just over ten years ago. I was in Kew Gardens, eager to see a new species of banana tree they were exhibiting when we literally bumped into each other. I offered to buy her a cup of tea in the gift shop café to apologize and we discovered we had both lived in Scotland."

Dodo took a sip. "Was she married before?"

"No, nothing like that. She was a governess."

"Golly, I had no idea. What family did she work for?"

He leaned back and pushed his finger through a droplet of water on the tabletop. "I don't know. She doesn't really talk about it. She was supposed to marry a successful accountant when she was young, but he died, and her useless brother wasted all the family money gambling, so she was forced to work. It is not a time in her life she cares to revisit."

The band members reappeared and started to play a popular tune.

"Would you like to dance, Lady Diantha?" Miles Penholland asked.

"Won't your wife mind?" she asked.

"Augusta does not like dancing," he replied. "She has gone to bed with a headache."

"In that case, I would be delighted," said Didi, taking Mr. Penholland's arm.

Rupert asked her mother to dance and Dodo sat and thought through her theory. The more she considered it, the more sense it made. And Rupert had said he loved her!

Mr. Penholland was animated in his conversation with Didi and she was laughing in response. *He must be enjoying time away from his sober, grave wife.*

When the dance was over, he brought Didi back to her chair and citing the late hour, excused himself rather abruptly.

Chapter 18

When Lizzie came to dress Dodo, there was an unmistakable twinkle in her eye. Though they were friends, Dodo understood better than most that there was still an invisible social line between a maid and her lady and wondered how she could bring up the subject of Mr. Scott without admitting to spying on them the evening before.

"You look very chipper this morning," Dodo said. "Enjoying the longer stay in Athens?"

Lizzie pursed her lips, trying to stamp out a grin.

"Oh, m'lady!" she began.

Dodo patted the bed and Lizzie sat next to her. "Ernie kissed me!"

"Tell me all about it!"

Lizzie divulged that they had been having lunch together each day and that they could barely drag themselves back to work. "We just never run out of things to say."

"I can imagine!" Dodo replied.

"So, the day after tomorrow is their last one in Athens, they are moving on to Egypt and Israel, and Ernie, Mr. Scott, asked me to meet him on one of the verandas last night, after he had settled his master in bed." Her eyes were flashing with the memories and her shoulders folded in. "It was so romantic, looking out at the lights and then he…kissed me. I almost melted, m'lady. I felt it all the way to my toes and back."

Dodo smiled. "I know exactly what you mean."

"And he asked for my address and has given me his. He's going to write to me every week." Lizzie clapped her hands together and settled them under her chin. "Can you believe it?"

"Absolutely!" replied Dodo. "He's an intelligent man who can see just what a gem you are."

Lizzie bit her lip. "Go on with you."

"Don't sell yourself short, Lizzie. You are one in a million. You totally deserve this!"

"I'll tell you one thing," she said, putting a hand on each cheek. "It was a million times better than the sloppy kiss I got in primary school!"

Detective Theodorou pushed through the door of the breakfast area and spying Dodo and Rupert, hurried over. Dodo was delighted to see that since she had last seen him, Theodorou had taken the time to shave. She was also eager to know all the details of the Goodweather interrogation.

"Lady Dorothea," he began, and nodded to Rupert. "Can we talk?"

"Of course!" She gestured for him to pull up a chair.

"I spent most of last evening interrogating the Goodweathers," he began. "I even put them in the jail overnight so that I could go home and get some sleep without having to worry they would vanish."

Dodo supposed the rules were different here. Such a thing would never pass muster in England.

"Did you find out anything useful? Have you arrested them?"

He ordered a bitter coffee and settled in.

"I have to tell you that last night I felt as though I was in one of those American movies. You know the kind, the detective is interrogating a suspect in a dark room with one light bulb swinging from the ceiling until the suspect can take it no more and confesses."

"Did one of them confess?" asked Rupert.

He sighed. "Alas, no. I spent hours questioning them individually but neither one broke, though the son withdrew into himself in a most alarming way. He is not very strong, that one." He leaned forward wagging a finger and Dodo could smell the cigarette smoke oozing from his jacket. "But keeping them overnight in jail, did the trick."

"They confessed?" she asked.

"Not to the murder, no. But to the charge of molestation in England, yes. Mr. Gerald Goodweather could see that his son was not handling the confinement well and they told me all about it early this morning."

Dodo dropped her fork to the table in a clatter. "Then you think they murdered Vera to keep their secret?"

Theodorou grabbed his chin. "Now, that is where it becomes rather complicated. Reginald claims it was not the Radford family where this alleged crime occurred, it was a family by the name of Chiswick and the girl in question was eighteen, not a child. He says they were in love."

"And you believe him?" she asked, trying to imagine any woman finding Reginald attractive.

"Heaven's no! But I've sent a telegram to the police station that investigated the situation in Kent. The thing is, I had to let them go this morning. Not enough evidence to hold them any longer, but I gave them a stern caution to stay at the hotel. If the return telegram corroborates their version, their motive disappears." The waiter placed the coffee on the table and Dodo watched as the detective drank it in one gulp. "If what they tell me is true, there is no connection to Miss Fenchurch."

Dodo slunk back against the back of her chair. She was angry at herself for assuming that the family in Kent where the incident with Reginald had taken place, was the same as the one Vera Fenchurch had worked for. She should have checked; it was an amateur mistake.

"What about the Cartwrights, I mean the Longbournes. Are *they* still in your custody?" she asked.

"No, that is why I am here. I brought them back to the hotel myself. They are not completely off the hook, but all things considered, the evidence against them is circumstantial. I have also asked them not to leave until I give my permission." He let out a discouraged sigh. "If the information from Kent proves that Reginald is not lying, I am back at square one." His jaw sagged and the bags under his eyes looked big enough to carry all his worries. "If both the Longbournes and the Goodweathers are vindicated, I am left with the Penhollands, and I have absolutely no evidence tying them to the crime at all. That promotion is slipping through my fingers. I need a miracle or two."

Dodo considered sharing her hunch about 'Gus but realizing that it wasn't hard proof she thought better of it. But *someone* had placed that hatpin under the mattress in the Longbourne's room, and she was more determined than ever to find out who.

"I'm sorry, detective. I'll keep thinking."

His face pinched like a child who cannot remember the answer on a test. "I fear that this crime may be headed for the 'unsolved' pile in the storage room." He pushed his chair back and winced as he stood. "Good day!"

As they watched him slouch his way out of the restaurant, Rupert exhaled loudly. "Dash it all! He's right. Whoever did this, might get away with it."

Dodo drummed the table. She had not failed a case yet and she did not mean to start with this one.

Didi slumped into the chair the detective had just vacated. "Gosh, I'm starving!" She caught the waiter's eye and he rushed to their table, almost tripping over his feet. She ordered some eggs and toast.

"Fancy some tennis later?" she asked them both.

Tennis was the last thing Dodo wanted to do. This case was getting the better of her and she just wanted to get all her thoughts down on a big sheet of paper. However, she did not want to spoil her sister's fun.

"Rather!" said Rupert with enthusiasm.

Problem solved! If the two of them played tennis, and they were much better suited for the game than she, it would give her the time to think.

"You two should play. I am happy to watch."

Rupert and Didi made arrangements to meet at the courts after breakfast.

"How was dancing with Mr. Penholland, last night?" Dodo asked her sister when their plans were settled.

"He was actually, quite entertaining," Didi said, fingering the flower arrangement in the middle of the table. "He has an amusing way with anecdotes. I know you don't like him, Dodo, but he's rather a dear, really."

"It's his wife I have no time for," corrected Dodo.

"She is a thorough battle-axe," agreed Didi.

"I don't know what he saw in her," said Rupert. "Always looks like she's sucking lemons."

"He actually told me about their meeting while we were dancing," Didi said. "She had been a nurse in Scotland before they met."

Dodo jerked her head. "A nurse? He told me she was a governess. Rupert, do you remember that?"

He narrowed his eyes over his teacup. "Yes, it was a governess because I thought how unlike my sister's governess she was."

The waiter sailed back and deposited Didi's plate on the table with a flourish.

"Could have been a slip of the tongue," said Didi, tucking into her eggs.

"Not really," contradicted Dodo. "A governess is responsible for the education of the older children who are instructed at home rather than a school. A nurse, on the other hand, is responsible for the care of the babies and toddlers. No one would make that mistake."

"Does it matter?" asked her sister.

Dodo tapped her lips. "I'm not sure." Fragments of conversations were rolling around in her head and she had the uncomfortable feeling that one of them was important. "I need to talk to Mummy again. I'll see you both later."

Dodo found her mother sitting on the balcony of her room, that overlooked the ever-present Acropolis.

After beating around the bush for a bit, Dodo asked, "Remember that family you told us about in Scotland that lost the child? Was it a baby by any chance?"

Her mother scrunched an eye. "Why? Is this about the murder? Oh, Dodo! Why are you getting involved? Leave it to the police."

Dodo's stomach squeezed with contrition. "I wish I didn't have to involve you, Mummy, but things are unraveling, and I have this odd, unfinished feeling in my chest that I think you might be able to fix for me. Can you please try to remember?"

She looked at Dodo with frustration. "I told you, I haven't seen Cynthia McTavish for years."

"Is that because of the tragedy?" Dodo persisted.

Her mother leaned back and closed her eyes. "I think it was. She withdrew and then we lost touch. It was the youngest boy. What was it?" Fine lines appeared all over Lady Guinevere's face as she reached into the far recesses of her mind. "He fell."

"That's good. Keep remembering."

"They lived by the coast…and he got away and fell over a cliff. Oh! How terrible. Fancy losing a child that way!"

Dodo moved to the drinks cabinet and poured her mother a comforting brandy.

"Here!"

Her mother took the drink and sipped it with frantic eyes. "He got away from the nurse and fell to his death. How does one go on after all that?"

Dodo did not know. But she did know that she did not want to put her mother through anymore. She had more than enough for David to use to look through the archives of the Times.

"I'm sorry, Mummy." She came and laid a blanket over her mother. "Take a nap and forget all about it."

"I think I shall," Lady Guinevere said, still sipping the brandy.

Dodo's father came into the room and noticing the anguished look on his wife's face went to her side. He cast an accusatory look in Dodo's direction.

"It was important, Daddy," she explained. "But I shall leave now."

She slipped from the room as her father whispered sweet nothings in her mother's ear.

Dodo leaned her back against the door. She felt guilty for spoiling an afternoon of her mother's holiday but now she was armed with the information she needed to move the case forward.

Chapter 19

As much as the telegram had changed human communication, in this new world of the telephone, telegrams were frustratingly slow and short. But international phone calls were the stuff of scientist's dreams and the telegram would have to do. Dodo had sent one off to David Bellamy as soon as she had left her parents' room and needed to do something active to take her mind off the waiting. She remembered that Didi had invited her to watch them play tennis.

Dodo was not the best player but she loved the outfits and had a weakness for men in their tennis whites. She wandered out to the tennis courts and found a comfortable place to sit. Didi was above average in her abilities and after just a few minutes Dodo could tell that Rupert was proving to be something of a whiz. Was he good at everything he tried? He was making Didi run from one side of the court to the other but he was hardly breaking a sweat. Dodo was more than content to admire his physique and lithe, athletic figure from afar.

After a particularly hard set, the two players retired to the table shaded by a large umbrella, where Dodo sat, and ordered some cold juice.

"Where did you learn to play like that?" asked Dodo of Rupert.

"Each summer when I came home from school, I took private lessons. My sisters did too. We are all pretty good, thanks to that."

"I also had private lessons," said Didi. "We both did." She looked in Dodo's direction.

"I'm still bally awful!" said Dodo with a laugh. "You two should play another game."

"I bet you are better than you think," replied Rupert. "My sister Beatrice used to send the ball to the moon and back."

"Oh, I used to," she said with a grin. "The tennis instructor would throw his hands in the air all the time. Don't you remember, Didi?"

"I do, but we both had a crush on him, so you wouldn't give up."

"Didi!" cried Dodo.

"Well, it's true!" she defended.

Dodo thought back to Philip Spencer, the youngish tennis instructor who had come to their home for four years. She wondered if she would think him handsome now. She glanced at Rupert who wore an impish smile.

"Falling for the tennis coach," he began. "Rather cliché, don't you think?"

"Absolutely!" she replied. "But he was rather dishy, and we were eager teens. It was a recipe for romance."

Didi knocked back the rest of her juice. "How about it, Rupert?"

"If you're sure you don't mind," he asked Dodo.

"Not at all. Go ahead."

They walked back to the court and Dodo leaned back in her chair and put her feet up. Perhaps she should take lessons again to make a better partner for Rupert. The idea wasn't too repulsive.

Rupert had a deadly serve that he tamed for Didi. That reflected well on him in Dodo's opinion. What did it say about a man who used brute strength without reserve to batter a woman in a sport? It was much kinder to rein in power in order to both enjoy a decent game.

As she enjoyed the loud thwack of the ball, a waiter came over, bearing something on a silver tray.

"For you, mademoiselle," he said with a bow.

A telegram! That was quick.

She opened it.

Greetings STOP ran over to the Times building after work STOP Aberdeen 1903 boy age 2 falls to death under care of nurse STOP Lavinia Farnsworth dismissed STOP Nanny accuses nurse of pushing child STOP nasty business STOP be careful STOP

At first glance this information did not seem to bear any relation to the situation here in Athens. She had hoped that it would prove to be the missing connection but felt let down. Unless…

Dodo ran back inside searching every floor of the tall hotel. She caught sight of Reginald skulking on the second floor but gave him a wide berth. She was finally rewarded with finding Miles Penholland sipping a cocktail and dozing on the top veranda, next to the open-air restaurant.

"Mind if I join you?" she asked, hailing a waiter.

Mr. Penholland opened his eyes with little enthusiasm but managed to rearrange his features into an insincere smile. Manners were a powerful force for human behavior.

"Of course, but I have to meet Augusta in a few minutes. I was just enjoying a bit of peace and quiet before joining her."

I bet she doesn't give you much of that.

"Cocktail, please," she told the waiter. "Peace and quiet?" she directed her question to Mr. Penholland.

"Augusta has been rather upset since the police told us we cannot go to Egypt. I needed a…break."

Just as I thought.

"Ahh," said Dodo as the waiter returned and she took a sip. "I expect they will let us leave soon," said Dodo.

"Oh?" said Mr. Penholland.

"The police just got some interesting news from London that I think will wrap up the case."

Without moving a muscle, Mr. Penholland said, "Is that so?"

"They now think this may all be connected to a tragedy some twenty years ago in Scotland."

"You have my attention, Lady Dorothea," he said, but his baggy cheeks gave the impression of complete disinterest.

"A family by the name of McTavish lost a little boy to a fall at the beach," she continued. "Have you heard of them?"

He shook his lethargic head. "Never."

"There was a nanny and a nurse in the employ of the house. The two-year-old boy fell, and the nurse was accused by the nanny of pushing the child over the cliff."

This piece of news inspired a small shiver. "How dreadful."

"The nurse was immediately dismissed, but in spite of the nanny's accusations, charges were never brought against her. The police think she moved from the area, changed her name, and started a new life."

"That would make sense," he murmured, looking at his watch with languid eyes. "I do apologize but I must get going. I told Augusta I would be back ten minutes ago." He stood and slowly lifted his white hat. "Let's hope this is all wrapped up soon so that we can be on our way. Good day, Lady Dorothea."

Dodo watched him waddle unsteadily through the tables and chairs to the elevator, not looking back once. She had hoped for more of a reaction, but he had seemed remarkably detached.

Perhaps she was wrong.

She waited until he had gone then took the elevator herself down to the lobby and called Detective Theodorou, to tell him about the cable.

"And *you* think that nurse from the incident in Scotland is the current Mrs. Penholland and that the nanny was Vera Fenchurch," he concluded.

"She is the only one of our party who fits the age," said Dodo. "But her husband was quite aloof when I mentioned it."

"Lady Dorothea," the detective began, his tone full of warning. "Was that wise to confront him, alone?"

"I was not alone, detective. I was in a public bar with waiters and other guests in the background. Besides Mr. Penholland is harmless enough. It is his wife that I suspect has a dark side."

"Stay put. I'm coming over right now," said the detective. "I shall be there in less than a quarter of an hour."

"Will do," she promised. "But perhaps I have been barking up the wrong tree from the beginning. Perhaps there was someone else *near* our group that Vera saw that day, who also went to the Parthenon. And there are other women at the hotel who are a similar age to Mrs. Penholland."

"And I shall be talking to all of them," agreed the detective. "Please don't go asking questions alone. You may put yourself in unnecessary danger."

The memory of other cases that had become perilous flooded her mind. "Don't worry, detective. I will be at the tennis courts with Rupert and my sister. But would you mind taking me with you when you question Mrs. Penholland and the other elderly ladies?"

There was a pause. "I suppose it is the least I can do since you have been so helpful. I'll see you soon."

She replaced the receiver slowly. She had been so convinced that Vera had recognized someone in their group that she had dismissed all other theories. It was a hotel, for goodness' sake! Full of people coming and going. It had been wrong to focus her attention so tightly on their group.

She wandered back to the reception desk.

"I wonder?" she said, flashing her brightest smile at the young desk clerk. "I have a rather extraordinary question."

"Of course," replied the clerk.

"How many women in their sixties are staying at the hotel?"

The young man's brow creased. "Let me check," he said opening the guest register. He ran a finger down the list. "Six," he said.

Dodo nodded. "Thank you!" She handed him a large tip, turning to go back out to the tennis courts.

Rupert and Didi were still playing but both of them now looked red and hot. She waved.

"Almost done!" Rupert shouted back. "Deuce!"

She took a seat at the table she had left and stared into space.

She had been so sure that the tale of tragedy in Scotland was the missing key. She had been like a dog following the scent of a bird, unable to see outside her own theory. She had turned the tables on innocent people just trying to enjoy a holiday. Guilt began to creep into her chest.

Rupert and Didi sank into the other chairs. "Golly! I'm hot now," declared Rupert who still had not so much as a hint of moisture on his brow. "How about a dip in the pool?"

"Oh, yes!" agreed Didi.

"Dodo, is something amiss?" he asked, with concern.

She exhaled. "I think I got this whole thing wrong again," she said.

"That would be a first," said Didi. "Why do you say that?"

She told them about the telegram and sharing the details with Mr. Penholland thinking he would recognize the story and exhibit some sort of reaction.

"There are six other women staying here that fit the age description." She put her face in her hands. "And in poking around I have exposed a perfectly innocent couple and had them thrown in jail during their honeymoon, and stirred up a scandal concerning the Goodweathers when they were making a great effort to put the past behind them. I'm a horrible person."

"Nonsense," said Rupert. "You say yourself that murder is a messy business."

"I do, don't I?" she said with a half-smile. "But this time I am responsible for much of the mess."

"Oh look!" said Didi. "Here is Detective Theodorou."

The grumpy detective had put on a clean, crisp suit. "Lady Dorothea, shall we?"

She almost declined in her present mood, but if this was all a giant wild goose chase, she could at least apologize to the Penhollands.

"Go!" encouraged Rupert. "You can find Didi and I at the pool after and tell us all about it."

As they stepped out of the elevator, Dodo caught sight of the back of Reginald Goodweather rounding a corner, his narrow shoulders hunched over. A grain of concern niggled at her brain.

They approached the Penholland's door and Detective Theodorou knocked three times.

"Perhaps they went out?" suggested Dodo.

"I checked," said the detective. "Their key is not in the lobby. Unless they too have fled, they are here."

"This is Detective Theodorou of the Athens police," he said in a raised, formal voice. "Please open the door." He put his ear to the wood and shook his head. Removing a key from his pocket that must have been the master, he inserted it in the lock and pushed it open an inch, declaring his title again.

Opening the door wide, he gasped, and Dodo pushed past him, charging into the room to see both Penhollands on their separate beds as if asleep. Her heart dropped off a cliff. 'Gus was a telltale shade of blue. Theodorou ran over to feel her pulse and said, "She's gone." Dodo raced to Mr.

Penholland and felt his neck. He was still warm and had a sluggish pulse. Between the beds on a nightstand were two glasses and a piece of paper.

She shook Miles Penholland by the shoulders and he moaned.

"I shall telephone for an ambulance," said the detective, running from the room. "But it is too late for his wife."

Dodo kept gently shaking Mr. Penholland, trying to rouse him from the effects of the drug. "Come on!" she murmured. "Come on!"

She tapped his cheeks with her palm and his eyes fluttered.

"Mr. Penholland," she said urgently. "Wake up!"

He groaned again.

Knowing there was nothing she could really do, she let go of him and grasping the fabric of her dress, lifted the glass. Tiny crystals were visible in the bottom. She placed it back on the nightstand and using her nails, she opened the paper that had been folded in two.

"To whom it may concern, it was me," the letter began. *"I, Miles Penholland, killed Vera Fenchurch. Augusta is innocent. She was ignorant of my actions and innocent of any part in the murder."*

Dodo dropped the paper. Miles Penholland? She *had* got it wrong. She picked up the paper again.

Vera recognized Augusta. Even after all these years.

Augusta's real name was Lavinia Farnsworth and she and Vera worked for the McTavish's twenty years ago. Augusta was innocent of the charges laid at her feet by Vera and was frantic that she would stir up old accusations and threaten the new life she had created. I settled her in the shade at the Parthenon to calm her nerves and went in search of Vera. I was just going to reason with her, but she was intent on telling her story unless I gave her money. The sun glinted on the lost hatpin as she ranted, and I snapped. I picked it up, thrust it in and left the woman to die, rolling her under tall grasses out of sight. It was all accomplished in the space of five minutes. Then I went back to Augusta as if nothing had happened.

Augusta did not ask me if I had killed Vera when the murder was announced. But when my wife told me that Lady Dorothea had mentioned that she believed the hatpin in the Cartwright's room to be planted, I began to worry and kept an eye on her. Then when the Cartwrights and Goodweathers were cleared, I felt the noose tighten. To top it off, I slipped up and mentioned to Lady Diantha that Augusta had been a nurse instead of a governess. I knew she would mention it to her sister who would put the pieces together like a terrier. Augusta would not be able to handle another scandal. The original had broken her. I met her shortly after she was released from a mental institution. I couldn't let that happen again.

She is at peace now. And I will join her shortly.

Chapter 20

The ornate lobby of *The Grand* was a flurry of activity.

"What will you do now?" Didi asked the people they knew as the Cartwrights. Frances' color was so much better now that she wasn't terrified of being outed. She had done her hair and make-up and looked very pretty. She gazed up at Matthew with adoration.

"We will go home, I think," he said. "This whole experience has shown us that there are worse things than our parents' disapproval. I am not ashamed of Frances, so why hide her?"

He directed his gaze to Didi. "I feel I must apologize," he said. "I rather leered at you when we first met in order to cement our lie that Frances and I were brother and sister."

"It made me so jealous!" declared Frances.

"Think nothing of it," said Didi. "Perfectly understandable given the circumstances."

"I still feel just horrible about getting you thrown in jail," said Dodo.

"It was our own fault, really," Frances assured her. "If we hadn't set up this whole deception in the first place, we would not have felt the need to run when Miss Fenchurch was killed."

"Jolly bad luck being in the middle of a murder, though," pointed out Rupert.

"It was, but if not for that, who knows how long we would have been on the run?" said Matthew. "Being in jail helped me see things straight. I love Frances and will face whatever my family can throw at me."

A porter came in and gestured to the newlyweds.

"Our taxi is here," he explained, lifting his bride from her chair. "Wish us luck."

"We wish you all the happiness in the world," said Dodo. "Perhaps we shall meet again."

Everyone kissed each other and then the Cartwrights, who were really the Longbournes but Dodo could not think of them as anything else, ran out the door and into the Mediterranean sunshine.

"It was very nice of them to forgive me for dragging them through hell and back," said Dodo, sipping a fresh lemonade.

"They are thoroughly nice people stuck in a difficult situation," said Rupert, reaching out to squeeze her hand.

"I don't think I would be so easy to forgive if you had sent *me* to jail," said Didi with a sunny laugh. "Especially not if I was on my honeymoon!"

Dodo took another refreshing sip as the Goodweathers entered the lobby, dressed in ordinary clothes. Reginald still looked shifty behind his thick lenses, but the relaxed smile made him appear less menacing. They wandered over.

"Off to Olympia?" asked Rupert.

"Heavens no!" said Mr. Goodweather. "We only have a passing interest in archeology and since everyone now knows it was a ruse, I think we will bury that persona."

"Where to then? Back home?" asked Dodo.

"Rumor is such a hard thing to outrun. And my boy here just had the bad luck to fall in love with the wrong girl. No, we are quite happy with our nomadic life for the time being."

"We are going to try our luck in the Holy Land. We've not done that yet," said Reginald with more enthusiasm than he had mustered all week.

"Well, have a jolly good time!" said Dodo.

The pair shook everyone's hands and left by the front door.

"Life is funny," said Didi. "People always seem to be running from youthful mistakes or trying to cover up new ones."

"Best not to make bad choices in the first place," said Dodo.

"But none of these people were actually in the wrong," said Rupert. "Vera Fenchurch was not even present when the tragedy occurred, according to the article Theodorou found. She had no evidence of wrongdoing but hurled the suspicion at Augusta Penholland anyway, and it crushed her. We shall never know why she thought Augusta would be capable of such a terrible act, I suppose."

"And the Cartwrights couldn't help that their families were at war. They did nothing wrong except to keep their families in the dark. I am sure their parents have been frantic, not knowing where they were. They will be so relieved to discover that they are alright, they will forgive them easily I would guess," said Didi.

"Let's hope so," said Dodo.

"And the Goodweathers have suffered at the hands of the rumor mill and an overprotective mother."

Detective Theodorou came through the main doors and seeing them, bustled over. "Just wrapping up loose threads," he explained. "I received a telegram from the police in Scotland who handled the child's death, and they explained that the boy who died was of a very difficult temperament. He had a bad temper and refused to sleep and would run Mrs. Penholland ragged. She would share her troubles with the nanny at night after the children were in bed and so Vera Fenchurch just put two and two together and made ten when the accident occurred. The other children testified that the boy was throwing a temper tantrum and ran away from the nurse, tripping over the cliff edge. A terrible tragedy for all involved."

"Thank you for telling us that," said Dodo. "We were just saying we might never know what spurred the hateful accusation."

"The Penhollands will be buried this afternoon if you are interested," said Theodorou. "Our custom is to bury quickly because of the heat."

Dodo inhaled, shaking her head. "No, thank you. I just want to forget the whole sorry business."

"Of course," replied the detective. "Are you leaving soon?"

"I believe my parents have contacted the captain of our yacht, and we will be leaving this afternoon. I can't wait to get away, if I'm honest."

"Well, it has been a pleasure working with you," said the detective taking her hand and kissing it. "When you return next year, do come and look in on me."

"Will do," said Dodo.

He waddled off as Dodo's parents appeared.

"Are you ready, darlings?" asked Lady Guinevere. "We are to set sail at three o'clock."

"I'll let Lizzie know," said Dodo. "Though I think she packed everything early to spend every last second with her beau."

At that very moment, Lizzie appeared on the arm of Ernest Scott, a smile as large as Sussex on her pretty lips.

"M'lady," she said, addressing Dodo's mother. "I should like you to meet Ernest Scott since he will be coming to the house often when we get back to England."

"Ohhhh!" squealed Dodo. "That is just the kind of good news I needed right now." She ran over to give him a hug but seeing the alarm in his dark eyes, stuck out her hand. "Welcome to the family," she said, turning to hug her maid.

"Now that we have made the official introductions, Ernest and I are going to find some lunch and say a temporary goodbye. I'll meet you at the dock at three. All the luggage is ready."

Dodo squeezed her maid again until she squeaked in protest that Dodo was crushing her ribs and then the affectionate pair walked off, hand in hand.

Dodo hugged herself. "I couldn't be happier for her," she declared like a proud mother.

"And she did it all without your interference," said her father with a grin. "Let's go and get lunch somewhere else before boarding."

Everyone agreed.

As they piled through the revolving doors, Dodo took one last look back. She doubted her mother would want to return to this particular hotel with its awful connection to the murders and suicides and she was alright with that. She was starting what she hoped was a new life with Rupert and beginning new traditions was more than appropriate.

"Come on," said Rupert, planting his soft mouth on hers. "Everybody's waiting."

The End...

Or did it end this way? Click on the link below for an alternate ending:

https://dl.bookfunnel.com/ecplboranj

Thanks for buying my book!

Ann Sutton

I hope you enjoyed this cozy mystery, *Murder on the Med*, and love Dodo as much as I do.

Interested in a free prequel to this series? Go to https://dl.bookfunnel.com/997vvive24 to download *Mystery at the Derby*.

Book one in the series, *Murder at Farrington Hall* is available on Amazon. https://amzn.to/31WujyS

"Dodo is invited to a weekend party at Farrington Hall. She and her sister are plunged into sleuthing when a murder occurs. Can she solve the crime before Scotland Yard's finest?"

Book two of the series, *Murder is Fashionable* is available on Amazon. https://amzn.to/2HBshwT

"Stylish Dodo Dorchester is a well-known patron of fashion. Hired by the famous Renee Dubois to support her line of French designs, she travels between Paris and London frequently. Arriving for the showing of the Spring 1923 collection, Dodo is thrust into her role as an amateur detective when one of the fashion models is murdered. Working under the radar of the French DCJP Inspector Roget, she follows clues to solve the crime. Will the murderer prove to be the man she has fallen for?"

Book three of the series, *Murder at the Races* is available on Amazon. https://amzn.to/2QIdYKM

"It is royal race day at Ascot, 1923. Lady Dorothea Dorchester, Dodo, has been invited by her childhood friend, Charlie, to an exclusive party in a private box with the added incentive of meeting the King and Queen. Charlie appears to be interested in something more than friendship when a murder interferes with his plans. The victim is one of the guests from the box and Dodo cannot resist poking around. When Chief Inspector Blood of

Scotland Yard is assigned to the case, sparks fly between them again. The chief inspector and Dodo have worked together on a case before and he welcomes her assistance with the prickly upper-class suspects. But where does this leave poor Charlie?

Dodo eagerly works on solving the murder which may have its roots in the distant past. Can she find the killer before they strike again?"

Book four of the series, *Murder on the Moors* is available on Amazon.

https://amzn.to/38SDX8d

When you just want to run away and nurse your broken heart but murder comes knocking.

"Lady Dorothea Dorchester, Dodo, flees to her cousins' estate in Dartmoor in search of peace and relaxation after her devastating break-up with Charlie and the awkward attraction to Chief Inspector Blood that caused it. Horrified to learn that the arch-nemesis from her schooldays, Veronica Shufflebottom, has been invited, Dodo prepares for disappointment. However, all that pales when one of the guests disappears after a ramble on the foggy moors. Presumed dead, Dodo attempts to contact the local police to report the disappearance only to find that someone has tampered with the ancient phone. The infamous moor fog is too thick for safe travel and the guests are therefore stranded.

Can Dodo solve the case without the help of the police before the fog lifts?"

Book five of the series, *Murder in Limehouse* is available on Amazon.

https://amzn.to/3pw2wzQ

Aristocratic star she may be, but when her new love's sister is implicated in a murder, Dodo Dorchester rolls up her designer sleeves and plunges into the slums of London.

Dodo is back from the moors of Devon and diving into fashion business for the House of Dubois with one of the most celebrated department stores in England, while she waits for a call from Rupert Danforth, her newest love interest.
Curiously, the buyer she met with at the store, is murdered that night in the slums of Limehouse. It is only of passing interest because Dodo has no real connection to the crime. Besides, pursuing the promising relationship that began in Devon is a much higher priority.

However, fate has a different plan. Rupert's sister, Beatrice, is arrested for the murder of the very woman Dodo conducted business with at the fashionable store. Now she must solve the crime to protect the man she is fast falling in love with.

Can she do it before Beatrice is sent to trial?

Book six of the series, *Murder on Christmas Eve* is available on Amazon.

https://amzn.to/3MvRUv6

Dodo is invited to meet Rupert's family for Christmas. What could possibly go wrong?

Fresh off the trauma of her last case, Dodo is relieved when Rupert suggests spending Christmas with his family at *Knightsbrooke Priory.*

The week begins with such promise until Rupert's grandmother, Adelaide, dies in the middle of their

Christmas Eve dinner. She is ninety-five years old and the whole family considers it an untimely natural death, but something seems off to Dodo who uses the moment of shock to take a quick inventory of the body. Certain clues bring her to draw the conclusion that Adelaide has been murdered, but this news is not taken well.

With multiple family skeletons set rattling in the closets, the festive week of celebrations goes rapidly downhill and Dodo fears that Rupert's family will not forgive her meddling. Can she solve the case and win back their approval?

For more information about the series go to my website at www.annsuttonauthor.com and subscribe to my newsletter.

You can also follow me on Facebook at: https://www.facebook.com/annsuttonauthor

About the Author

Agatha Christie plunged me into the fabulous world of reading when I was 10. I was never the same. I read every one of her books I could lay my hands on. Mysteries remain my favorite genre to this day - so it was only natural that I would eventually write my own.

Born and raised in England, writing fiction about my homeland keeps me connected.

After finishing my degree in French and Education and raising my family, writing has become a favorite hobby.

I hope that Dame Agatha would enjoy Dodo Dorchester at much as I do.

Acknowledgements

My proof-reader – Tami Stewart

The mother of a large and growing family who reads like the wind with an eagle eye. Thank you for finding little errors that have been missed.

My editor – Jolene Perry of Waypoint Author Academy

Sending my work to editors is the most terrifying part of the process for me but Jolene offers correction and constructive criticism without crushing my fragile ego.

My cheerleader, marketer and IT guy – Todd Matern

A lot of the time during the marketing side of being an author I am running around with my hair on fire. Todd is the yin to my yang. He calms me down and takes over when I am yelling at the computer.

My beta readers – Francesca Matern, Stina Van Cott,

Your reactions to my characters and plot are invaluable.

The Writing Gals and 20Booksto50k for their FB author community and their YouTube tutorials

These sites give so much of their time to teaching their Indie author followers how to succeed in this brave new publishing world. Thank you.

Printed in Dunstable, United Kingdom